A Saga of Sisters and Secrets

Nellie Brooks

Merpaper Press LLC

CONTENTS

Edited by Karen Meeus Editing

Published by Merpaper Press LLC

CHAPTER 1

"The property didn't look this run-down last October. How can six months make that much difference?" Christy leaned against her car, her eyes tracing the worn edges of her dilapidated seaside cottage. She managed a weak smile as she turned to face her new neighbor.

"Think of it as a diamond in the rough." Billie shielded her eyes from the bright May sun of a Mendocino Cove afternoon. "After all, the house has been standing empty for years." She glanced at Christy. "It always needed a splash of paint and a few roof shingles. But you knew that when you bought it."

Christy sighed, feeling fatigue etch across her face in new wrinkles and lines. She had only just arrived in the small coastal town of Mendocino Cove, and already she felt bone-tired. The weariness from the long, lonely drive over the mountains mingled with the burden of a never-ending conga line of emergencies that had danced through her life. The last six months had aged her more than all her sixty-five years before.

"In my head, the cottage was almost ready to move in. Not perfect, but good enough to spend a quiet night by the sea," she admitted. Clearly, in her head, the cottage had become more than it was.

Billie cleared her throat, and when she glanced over, there was a mischievous glint in her eyes. "You *can* spend the night. I mean, right after you work a little magic on the plumbing. Unless...I mean, the sea is *right there*." She grinned, her good mood clearly unaffected by Christy's poor attitude.

Christy didn't bother pondering what exactly the younger woman was insinuating. Instead, she brushed back one of her short silver curls. "What do you think about the roof?"

The corners of Billie's lips dropped as she appraised it. "It's not going to fall down anytime soon. But I'd repair the dark patches if you want to stay dry and keep out the mold. Obviously, the chimney needs a good sweep by someone who knows what they're doing, and, uh...well, and so on. Come on, Christy, cheer up." Billie smiled bracingly. "It's nothing you can't handle. You were brimming with excitement about sprucing up the place last fall."

"I know. But that was last fall," Christy murmured. She was keenly aware that she should be grateful to own a seaside cottage at all, no matter the condition. But she was too exhausted to fight the urge to whine. And terribly homesick for her old place and her old life. For thirty busy years, she had loved her life in San Francisco, where she had lived in one of the elegant historic gems gracing the heart of the city.

Buying the small cottage in Mendocino Cove had been an impulsive decision. Renovating it was supposed to be a fun exercise in bright fabrics and quick-drying paints. Something to keep her busy as she eased fully into retirement. A chance at flipping her very own fixer-upper, just to see if she could. A way to stay in shape without having to go to the gym and swing kettlebells in front of twenty-year-olds in spandex.

But all that was over. Now, the cottage was her only refuge. A secret hide-out to lick her wounds.

Pulling herself together, Christy locked the car and crossed the street for a closer look at her newest problem.

Billie kept pace. "I heard about what happened with your city apartment. Wait, let's go down here." She waved for Christy to come, leading the way down an overgrown stone path. "I'm sorry your landlord in the city decided to sell so suddenly. He should've given you more warning."

"He got a cancer diagnosis and decided to spend the rest of his retirement checking off his bucket list. I don't like it. But I do understand." Christy spread her arms, the gesture all-encompassing.

Billie smiled. "But maybe it was a blessing in disguise. Just wait until you see the view in the back. Come this way, it's easier. Mind the brambles there."

Christy followed gingerly, carefully choosing where she stepped. At her age, bones turned brittle, and a fall was no joke. Unfortunately, the ground was barely visible. Weeds and vines seemed to have devoured what was once a trail, sparing only a glimpse at a paving field stone here and there. Lone stems of lavender and single blossoms of roses, witnesses of a long-ago time when the yard was still tended, peeked out of the weeds. When Billie unexpectedly stopped halfway around the cottage, Christy almost ran into her. "Oops! I'm sorry."

"There. Look." Beaming, Billie pointed ahead. "Isn't that something else?"

Christy lifted her head, her eyes widening as she took in the view that was opening behind the house. "Yes," she admitted, suddenly feeling her muscles relax and her lungs expand. "You're right, Billy. That is something else."

Decades of appraising precious art for a big auction house in San Francisco had intimately acquainted Christy with every detail of line, color, and composition. Yet even she had to shake her head in wonder at the majesty of the Pacific Ocean that stretched to the horizon like a lustrous tapestry woven in silk and silver.

Not far out, low cliffs directed the wild sea into a small, sweet cove. Despite the balmy breeze, the water remained calm, only occasionally sending a glassy wave to lap at the shore like some wonderfully fantastical beast checking on its treasure.

Among the three cottages nestled along the coastline, this one boasted a sliver of beach. A handful of long strides would bring Christy down the grassy slope of the backyard and into the fine, golden sand. Old as she felt, she was sorely tempted to take those strides.

"I mean, just think about enjoying all this while you're drinking your coffee here in the mornings," Billie noted pragmatically, clearly better used to the view. "Perfectly private too. If you don't mind the pelicans giving you the side eye, nothing's stopping you from sitting on the beach in your robe or your PJs, or heck, sit here naked if you like. It's your home and your castle now, isn't it?" She scratched her arm. Then she thoughtfully added, "Though to be honest, we do get a lot of fog in the morning, and it can be cool. You might not see much sitting out here until the sun burns it up. Still. It's not nothing."

"I wouldn't mind the pelicans," Christy said. Sheepishly, she added, "I did the right thing after all, snapping up this little gem, didn't I?" If she didn't feel so numb and down on her luck, she'd probably be as ecstatic about her impulse purchase now as she'd been when she signed the papers last fall.

"Of course you did. I promise that the cottage wouldn't have lasted a second longer on the market," Billie assured her. "You were in the right place at the right time. Once you're done with the improvements, you'll have yourself the best little retirement home anyone can dream up."

"I bet you're right." Christy didn't like to be reminded of her retirement. But she needed to come to terms with it. Her former life of working in the urban glitz and glam of the high-stakes art world was over.

"So you like it again now?" Billie smiled knowingly, as if she had foreseen Christy's reaction to the glorious backyard view.

"I do. I love it," Christy replied, trying to sound as enthusiastic as possible. Her insides had been like a block of ice when she arrived, but the beauty of her surroundings was beginning to melt the edges of her chilled heart, thawing off drops one by one.

Christy shifted her stance as finally, a sense of new beginning dawned on her. She took a breath of the salty air, able to fully inhale for the first time in months. "I really do," she said, letting it go again with an audible whoosh. "This view makes my soul expand and...well. You know." Embarrassed, she broke off. Maybe her down-to-earth neighbor would think she was being woo-woo if she talked about her soul expansion and thawing heart and all that.

But Billie's smile only deepened. "I feel the same. Doesn't the air taste better here?"

Christy nodded. There was the scent of the ocean that she loved, salt and kelp and sand and barnacles. But mingled in were also the sweet fragrances of honeysuckle, roses, and lavender. Searching for the source, she scanned the knee-deep weeds that surrounded them. "What smells so good? I don't see many flowers."

"They are here somewhere," Billie promised. "Like, over there." She pointed at the remnants of a patio that was surrounded by a low, tumble-down wall of fieldstones and shielded by a few old trees.

Christy squinted. "I may not be a gardener, but those are all weeds sprouting around the cottage."

"Oh dear." Billie laughed at the statement. "Never mind. I'll help you clean up the garden so you don't accidentally pull out the good stuff because there's plenty." She squatted and pulled a large pink blossom out from under a cover of bright-green vines. "Look at this peony. All it wants is a bit of weeding and a sturdy stake." Gently, she replaced the heavy flower and straightened again. "Luckily for you, ma'am, I love gardening. And I've always wanted permission to tackle this lot."

"Well, you certainly have it. And it's very kind of you to offer." Christy loved peonies as much as the scent of the sea but was used to seeing them in—or even better, painted on—antique vases. "I always thought I'd like to garden in my old age. But I've lived in cities most of my life and wouldn't even know where to start."

"I'll show you the ropes," Billie promised cheerfully. "Like I said, I've been waiting to get my hands on this mess ever since you bought the place. But I didn't want to presume."

"Zero presumption, Billie. I'd love to learn from you. Now, the house...hmm." Christy pulled the jacket of her designer suit tighter around her and turned to face her new home.

When she bought the cottage, Christy had been full of life and confidence, eager for the project. She pictured herself painting walls in the flickering light of the fireplace and planting hydrangeas. Maybe strike out and turn the small shed into a studio where she could learn to refinish furniture or throw pottery on the wheel or something like that. For weeks, images of herself wearing breezy overalls and sneakers, a bandanna holding back her hair, had filled her head. Naturally, she owned none of those clothing items. Her wardrobe was full of the tailored business suits and high heels she'd worn in the city, and her haircut was expensive enough to stay in place without clips or clasps, let alone hippy-dippy dream bandannas.

Then everything changed, and it changed quickly.

As soon as Christy returned to San Francisco after signing the closing papers, one bad thing had chased the next. The stress zapped all the energy and courage she'd so arrogantly assumed were her birthright.

It started when her best friend, with whom she was in constant contact and met at least once a week over dinner, had suddenly succumbed to an undiagnosed heart disease. They'd been the same exact age. They even had their birthdays in the same month.

Christy was still reeling from grief when her auction house invited her to evaluate an antique oil painting. Even though she was already retired and no longer employed, she still worked for them as a consultant on a freelance basis.

Distracted, she had missed the signs of a clever forgery and given her stamp of approval. It didn't take long for the competition to gleefully point out the mistake. In a business where reputation was everything,

Christy had committed the fatal twin sin of embarrassing her company and costing it money.

Immediately after the scandal blew up, calls from colleagues and artists dwindled to a trickle. Soon enough, they dried out entirely.

As if that wasn't enough, her landlord of several decades was diagnosed with early prostate cancer and sold Christy's building. He'd barely left the state in his brand-new RV, bound for every national park known to man, when the corporate company that now owned the building sent a letter, formally announcing a slew of modernizations. Almost none of the tenants could afford the astronomic increase in cost. In a vague staging of protest, they all decided to move out together. But the company either didn't notice or didn't mind. People who had lived next door to each other for decades were ripped apart, each trying to rearrange their lives and housing as best they could.

In one fell swoop, Christy had lost her best friend, her reputation, her source of income, her home, and her neighborly support system.

"Are you okay?" Billie asked gently, calling Christy back to the present.

"Sure. I'm fine," she said, trying to keep her voice steady. She fought hard against feeling like a victim. In the end, she still had so much. Much more than others. But the helpless feeling that it was all unfair still crept up on her sometimes. Especially when she was exhausted.

"You can stay somewhere else until the renovations are done, can't you?" Billie sounded cautious. "Do I remember Agatha saying something about that?"

"She very kindly offered me the use of her spare room." Christy checked the slim watch on her wrist. "Actually, she might be waiting for me to arrive."

Agatha was one of the last friends Christy had from the olden days. She was also the owner of the cove's third little cottage and the other new neighbor. "I should have come up more often to visit with her. But I was...busy," Christy added guiltily. She had not been *busy*. More like depressed. Down in the dumps. Sitting on the sofa, watching mysteries without paying a lick of attention.

"That's all right," Billie replied, as if she had been able to hear Christy's thoughts. "Do you have friends who are going to come and help you renovate?"

Christy hadn't even considered that possibility. "No, I don't think so. Not anymore." Christy walked to the patio door. It was locked from the inside. She took a few steps back and put her head into her neck to look up at the white gable of her cottage.

The sun shone bright and warm in a sky that was the translucent blue of an enormous aquamarine. The breeze played with Christy's short hair, gently cooling her, and clouds as puffy and white as lambs sailed over the house. It made it look like the gable was moving toward her in an everlasting bow of greeting.

Without meaning to do it, Christy felt the corners of her lips tug upward. She shook her head, surprised to find that for the first time in a long while, a genuine smile was spreading over her face.

She would replace the weathered, cracked shingles up there, rebuild the welcoming front porch and put up wide white wicker chairs, and splurge on a collection of terracotta pots spilling over with sun-drenched bougainvilleas and roses and hydrangeas. She rubbed a hand over her cheek and turned back to the younger woman. "You know, Billie, I do see it again, all that potential. It's slowly coming back to me."

"Right? I'd paint the outside in coastal colors," Billie said critically. "Perhaps a soft blue or sea-foam green. Definitely use a sea-glass palette."

"That sounds nice." Suddenly, Christy remembered an aquarelle she had valued many years ago. It hadn't been very valuable or precious or even particularly special, but she'd never forgotten the tranquil coastline with gentle waves lapping against the shore. The artist had captured the subtle play of sunlight on the water, the rhythm of the waves, and the wild beauty of a summer spent by the sea.

"I think I've just found my inspiration," Christy said, surprised at the vision that had appeared before her inner eye. She reached out and touched the old white wood of the cottage. It was warm, and dry, cracked from sun and storms and time. Barely audible, she hummed a greeting under her breath. Because surely it was just as woo-woo as talking about soul expansion and thawing hearts to say, *Hey there, old house. We'll start this new life together, you and I, won't we?*

"At this stage, the possibilities are endless," Billie said softly. "Let yourself dream."

Christy nodded. She'd widen the windows to allow plenty of natural light to flood the interior. Flowing, gauzy curtains to play with the breeze and soften the moonlight at night. Gleaming hardwood floors to witness the passage of time, cozy, overstuffed sofas and chairs in bright floral patterns by a fireplace. Bookshelves, as full of art and framed photos as they were of her books.

Potted plants, her sculptures and vases and aquarelles, a rustic farmhouse kitchen with white cabinets and an island for cooking and entertaining. Upstairs, a big, comfortable bed in front of a panoramic window. She'd see the Pacific last thing at night and first thing in the morning, and when she couldn't sleep and was lonely, at least the moonshine swimming in the water would keep her company. A claw-footed tub in the bathroom and guest rooms ready for in case her former friends managed a visit after all.

Overwhelmed by the stream of ideas, Christy let go of the house and stepped back. "I'm depressed," she said, surprising herself again. "But the house is poking pin pricks into the gray shell around me."

"Seaside cottages have a way of cheering you up, don't they?" Billie nodded. "You should get some nice wicker chairs out here. Something comfortable so you can sit and watch the sun go down." She tilted her head in question and smiled. "Doesn't the thought of that add another pin prick in your shell?"

"I don't mean to come across as ungrateful or spoiled, Billie, though I'm afraid that at this point in my life, I'm a little of both." Christy smiled back. "Thank you for coming over to say hi, my dear. Thank you for putting up with my whining and complaining about moving here. I promise I'm not always like this. I promise I'll grow a better attitude."

Billie nodded. "It takes time to build a new life," she said. "Starting over is never easy, not even when you get a cottage by the sea into the bargain. But if there's one thing we have a handle on here in Mendocino Cove, it's getting people on their feet again."

"Then I'm in the right place. I could use some of your magic." Christy lowered her vintage shades from her head onto her nose. "I honestly didn't think I'd have such a rough time of it. Retirement, aging, saying goodbye to old friends..." She stopped herself abruptly. Looking back did no good. Like a lover who'd grown bored and moved on, her old life was done with Christy. It was time for her to be done with it too.

Billie chuckled. "Let's start your new life with a nice slice of cake and a cup of hot coffee. Should we go see Agatha?"

"Definitely." Christy nodded, firmly squelching any alarm over staying at her eccentric friend's tiny place. They would arrange themselves. They had done it before. Though never for long.

Now Billie laughed openly at her. "If she gets irritable, you can always crash with me. Or you can rent a room at the hotel in the forgotten cove. You have a car, so the distance won't be a problem."

"Thank you, Billie. It's good to know I have options in case I outstay my welcome," Christy said. "I guess I didn't realize the hotel had reopened already." The picturesque historic mansion was a local landmark, renowned for its old-world charm and fine, sandy beach. It had stood empty for many decades and only started to undergo a renovation a few months ago.

"Yes, it's almost all done. The hotel is gorgeous, and I'm sure they'll give you a prime room at a prime rate just for the asking." Billie leaned over a bunch of ragged bushes springing up between fieldstones to pluck a sprig of bright purple lavender. She crushed the tiny blossoms between her fingers, releasing a burst of fragrance into the salty air.

Christy inhaled the soothing aroma. "I'm so glad. I was truly worried about imposing too much on Agatha," she admitted. "It could easily be a few months before I can move into the cottage."

Billie opened her hand and let the crushed lavender sail to the ground. "Nah," she said and rubbed her palms clean. "It'll be done in no time. By the way, don't count on Agatha growing tired of you anytime soon. I think she's actually really looking forward to having you stay with her. She baked all day yesterday to welcome you."

"She made me one of her lemon cakes?" Christy smiled. Agatha was famous for lemon cakes, and rightly so. They were very good indeed—juicy and plump and citrusy, with a sweet glaze that melted in your mouth.

Billie's eyebrows rose. "She made a lot more than a lemon cake, Christy. Agatha might pretend she's a tough old cookie, but I don't think you understand how happy she is that you're going to move to Mendocino Cove. Come on. Let's go meet her."

CHAPTER 2

"Christy!" Agatha was standing in the door, wearing a flour-dusted apron and clutching a huge, fluffy cat in her arms.

Reaching out of the open driver's window to wave, Christy parked her dark-blue convertible. Billie followed suit in her old red pickup truck, and both women got out.

"Agatha!" Christy opened her arms to hug her sister of the heart. The massive cat opened a pink mouth full of needle-sharp teeth, flattened its ears, and hissed. "Oh." Startled, Christy stepped back. A tuft of long hair floated through the air, settling on her sleeve. She picked it off and released it in the breeze. But instead of taking it away, the breeze blew it back, glomming it more firmly onto the same sleeve as if to say, *Leave it. That's where it goes.*

Cackling, Agatha patted the monster. "Never mind, Christy, I'm covered head to toe in cat hair too! Gordon sheds a little, but he's really a sweet kitten. He can be a tad possessive though. So watch out."

Christy raised an eyebrow. "Possessive over what?"

Agatha shrugged. "Me, his food, his toys, a glass on the table...it changes. You never know."

So basically, the cat attacked whomever, whenever. "Cute." Christy glanced at Billie, who was grinning from a respectful distance.

"But he's just a big cuddler," Agatha insisted and let the cat go. It jumped to the ground in a whirlwind of hair, staring back at his mistress with an offended look on his squashed face. "Shoo! Go sit in the sun and enjoy yourself," Agatha said and brushed off her hands. "I can't hold you every single minute of the day." She turned to Christy. "Being in the shelter has traumatized him, poor baby. He needs a lot of love and affection. Don't worry. You'll love him."

"There's hair everywhere." Billie fanned the air in front of her face.

It was Agatha's turn to open her arms. "Welcome to my humble abode, kiddo!" Without further ado, she threw her arms around Christy. She smelled of cat, and wood smoke, and something sweet baking in the oven.

Gingerly, Christy patted her friend's back. "Hello, my dear. Thank you so very much for inviting me to stay with you until... I'll do my best to...well. I'll just do my best. Full stop."

"We'll be as snug as a bug in a rug," Agatha promised.

"Of course we will." Christy pulled away to study her friend.

Like her, Agatha was getting on in years. But she took to it differently. Her weathered face had never seen sunscreen or retinol, her hips had never been molded by diets, and her hair hung in a wind-blown, kitchen-sheared salt-and-pepper bob onto her shoulders. But she made it look good. Agatha's blue eyes sparkled, her grip was strong, and her lips smiled widely as she took Christy's hand and pulled her into the house.

"Right. Billie, are you coming in?" Agatha called over the shoulder. "I have cake!"

Billie laughed. "Uh, no, I just wanted to say hi and make sure you're home. I should get back though; I need to feed my new patient."

Christy looked back. "Patient? What patient?"

"A cormorant," Billie explained, already turning away. "Doing my bit to save the world, one broken wing at the time."

"Oh." Christy nodded, remembering now that Billie ran a small marine rescue station. "That's very good of you."

"You wouldn't believe how much cormorants can eat. Well, good luck, you two!" Billie waved a quick goodbye, and then she went to her truck.

"Good luck? Who says that? She should've said 'have fun,' or 'enjoy your cake.' I did bake us something nice." Agatha shut the door and pointed at an accordion row of hooks on the wall, the old pine wood dark with age and use. "You can hang your jacket there."

Christy looked down at her expensive suit. "You're not supposed to take off the jacket," she said, unsuccessfully trying once again to brush off the tuft of hair.

Half of it sailed from her sleeve and landed on her skirt. She sighed. "It's part of the outfit."

"Well, then leave it on, I guess. But not the shoes." Agatha went ahead, disappearing into the house.

Christy knew the drill. Under the coat rack, she spotted the same wide felt slippers, downtrodden at the heel, that she'd worn last time. She stepped out of her ballet flats—tan with iconic black toe caps—and into the slippers. Catching her reflection in the hall mirror, she stopped short.

The sea breeze had tousled her hair frizzy. In the relative dark of the entrance corridor it no longer looked silver and sleek, but white and wiry. The flecks of cat hair made her clothes look shabby, and the pencil skirt looked altogether silly and out of place with the old wide slippers. Christy's usually pale cheeks were flushed a ruddy red from the heat of the sun. Her makeup had worn off, showing the lines of exhaustion as well as the gray shadows and bags under her eyes that came from the many sleepless nights of the last months.

Christy barely recognized herself. In the rough tumble from the peak of her adult life, she'd undergone a physical transformation.

"Where are you?" Agatha called from the kitchen. "Hurry up! The tea is getting cold!"

"Coming! I'm coming, Agatha." Raking her fingers through her hair, Christy scuffled—the slippers didn't allow any other gate—into the kitchen. Of all the rooms in her friend's cottage, she liked the kitchen best. It was the biggest room in the house and a vibrant hub, full of vintage utensils, framed recipes, and open shelves full of spices, potted flowers, family photos, and clearly beloved, dog-eared cookbooks. A worn wooden table with a vase full of blooming rhododendrons served as the home's gathering place.

"Aha, there you are." Agatha pointed at the earthenware teapot on the counter. A trail of fragrant steam rose from the nozzle. "I hope you don't mind peppermint. My stomach was a little upset earlier, and peppermint is supposed to help."

"Oh no. I'm sorry to hear that." Grateful as Christy was to be able to stay with her friend, sharing the tiny bathroom with an upset stomach would be inconvenient.

Unbothered herself, Agatha turned to pull something from the fridge. "Nothing a nice slice of cream torte won't fix," she said confidently. "Don't worry, I'm sure it's not catching."

"Excellent. Good." It hadn't even occurred to Christy that a bug might be going around. Being sick in someone else's house would be even more inconvenient than sharing the bathroom.

"Ha-ha, I know your knees are trembling that you'll catch it." Agatha set whatever she had in her hands on top of the stove, her back covering the view. "Don't worry, I'm not sick. I've just had too much coffee and tea."

"Then have some water, Agatha. Flush the caffeine out." Christy had only moderate trust in her friend's diagnostic powers.

"That's not how it works."

"Right." Christy let it go. "It smells good." Shuffling to the counter, she carefully picked up the heavy, hot teapot and brought it to the table, where she poured the steaming tea into the two waiting, mismatched mugs. She sat and pulled one of the mugs close, eyeing Agatha's back. "What did you bake?"

"I wanted to try something new, but I couldn't decide what. So I made a bunch." Agatha turned, presenting a cake covered in a smooth, glossy chocolate ganache and decorated with fresh raspberries. She put the plate on the small kitchen island. "Chocolate raspberry," she declared. "It was an experiment."

"It looks fantastic." Christy inhaled the rich, luscious scent. "Does it have gluten?"

"Of course it has gluten in it, silly. It has flour, eggs, butter, sugar, all the good stuff." Agatha opened the double-wide fridge again and pulled out another torte. This one was already missing a sampler chunk when she showed it. "I'm extremely fond of this one. It's a lemon-blueberry mascarpone torte."

It was warm in the kitchen, and Christy took off her jacket after all, hanging it over the back of her chair. Suddenly, it hardly mattered whether she was put together or not. "Is mascarpone what's the matter with your stomach?" she asked kindly.

"Possibly," Agatha replied archly, not even trying to defend her caffeine theory. "I'll have to eat another slice to check."

"Fight fire with fire," Christy agreed.

"Where...oh!" Agatha left the kitchen through the door that led, as Christy remembered, into Agatha's lean-to greenhouse, and returned a moment later with a third creation. "I also found this recipe for a pistachio and rose water torte and couldn't resist."

Christy's eyes widened. "It looks beautiful, but that makes three enormous tortes between the two of us, my dear." Only once in a blue moon did Christy allow herself to buy a pastry at her favorite bakery. Usually, in the name of her health and waistline, she stuck to protein and vegetables. Hopefully, Agatha wouldn't be offended if Christy only sampled the rich delicacies. Otherwise, the mascarpone and chocolate ganache might pull a number on Christy's stomach too.

"Eating a lot of cake is a good thing, Christy." Agatha pulled two plates from a cupboard and, without having to look, pulled a cake server from a drawer. "You know I like to bake. What else is there to do?"

"What is there besides baking? Books, I suppose. Art. Conversations with friends." Christy smiled. "Mind you, I'm not complaining about you baking; I'm sure it's all dangerously delicious. But just so you know, I mean to take you out to dinner every day."

Agatha looked satisfied with the compliment. "Nonsense, my dear, nobody's going out. We'll cook something nice right here at home." She lifted the cake server. "Which one do you want first?"

"I'll try the pistachio and rose torte, please," Christy said, swallowing her usual *but only a really small slice.* Agatha must have planned and shopped and baked for hours, and Christy couldn't bring herself to dampen her obvious joy.

"Here." Agatha laid a beautifully green-and-pink marbled slice on Christy's plate. For herself, she cut a large slice from the mascarpone creation, which looked like it consisted of light and fluffy lemon-infused layers sandwiched between velvety mascarpone and juicy blueberry filling.

"Let's sit outside," Agatha suggested. Without waiting for a response, she grabbed her plate and mug and led the way out of the kitchen.

Glad to get another glimpse of the stunning scenery, Christy picked up her own welcome meal and followed her friend outside, where there was a small patio with Adirondack chairs. She awkwardly lowered herself into the deep bucket seat while balancing her food and drink, glad her hips and lower back did not complain too much. "Ah." She leaned back. Once seated, it was very comfortable. Even if her knees rose at an unladylike angle toward the sea. "It's so pretty here."

Well past noon, the sun was descending the aquamarine sky. Below, the ocean lay still and calm, waiting for the sun to arrive. Like at Christy's own property, grass gently sloped to the edge of the sea. But instead of the weeds and vines at her cottage, blooming rhododendrons and bougainvilleas and roses grew here. "Hey." Christy tried to lean forward in the deep bucket seat with little luck. "Can you see my house from here?"

"Only if I go all the way down to the water." Agatha pointed with her spoon. "Same with Billie's cottage. I like it. Private, but if you need an egg or something, you can just sort of wave at your neighbor. One wave, sugar. Two, eggs. Three, it's something else entirely."

"You could also just use your phone," Christy said and balanced her plate on her knees. "Because what if the other person isn't standing by the water right the moment you need sugar? And how do they know how much sugar?"

"It's true, mostly we just use the phone," Agatha admitted contentedly. "I mean, always. We never wave. We could, though, if we phoned first to arrange it. I could work out a system if we wanted one."

"That's all right." The alluring scent of Christy's torte was becoming distracting, and suddenly, she felt ravenous. She sank her spoon into the luscious layers and tasted Agatha's creation. "Hmm." The delicate layers of pistachio-flavored cake were covered in rose water-infused frosting that was generously sprinkled with more crushed nuts and edible petals. "Agatha, this is incredible," she said, for once ignoring the rule about not talking and chewing at the same time. "Where do you even find these ingredients? Rose water? Rose *petals*? Can you buy that at the supermarket?"

"I don't think so. At least not the petals," Agatha replied and pointed at a bush of blooming roses that grew up the side of the lean-on. "It's not exactly hard to pick them yourself."

"It's delicious," Christy declared and took two more bites than she had meant to. And another one, for good measure. And one more nibble.

"Have you had lunch?" Agatha asked, peering at her. "Or even breakfast? You look like you've lost a lot of weight."

"I didn't," Christy admitted. "At my age, you don't have much of an appetite anymore."

"Isn't that the same age I am?" Agatha finished her slice and sighed happily. "Because my appetite seems to be doing just fine."

Christy glanced at her friend. "You're right. It's not the age; that's just what I tell people because I can't tell them that I'm depressed. But I suppose I can tell you." She set down her empty plate. "You know everything that has happened in the last six months. It's why I have no appetite and can't sleep. This is the most I've eaten in days."

"Well, that's no good. We'll have to change it." Agatha put a hand to her stomach and frowned. "Oh."

Alarmed, Christy looked over. "What?"

"Excuse me for a moment." Agatha hauled herself out of her chair and went inside. By the time she returned, the blue sky had turned the color of the lavender blooming by Christy's cottage, and the wind had picked up.

"Are you all right there?" Christy had been dozing, but now she realized she was getting cold. She heaved herself out of her deep chair. "How are you feeling?"

"I don't know," Agatha said. "But I took something to calm down my stomach." She rubbed her arms. "It's cooled down. Let's sit inside and make a fire for the evening." Her stomach gurgled, and she put her hands on it.

"I'm not hungry for dinner," Christy said as she collected their plates and mugs. It would be better for Agatha not to top up the rich tortes already in her belly. "Actually, if you don't mind, I think I'd love to go to bed. I feel like I could sleep now."

Her friend nodded. The big cat had returned and was slinking around her legs, purring loudly. Agatha picked it up. "Me too. We'll have the fire tomorrow."

Christy went to get her suitcase from the car, then brushed her teeth in the tiny bathroom and wiped off the last of her makeup. Under the foundation, her skin was pale, and there were gray shadows under eyes, witnesses of the many nights where she'd lain awake instead of sleeping. Taking her cosmetics bag with her, she returned to the small bedroom. It only had a bed, a dresser with shallow drawers, and a window looking out at the sea, but it was all she wanted or needed. Outside, the sun was just kissing the ocean, making it blush a fiery golden red.

Christy stood by the window for a while, looking out at the sea. She was tired, and now that it was quiet, her mind was suddenly whirling, trying to catch up with the stream of images and impressions the day had brought. Billie laughing, Agatha waving, the rich, good food. But also finding her way alone over rolling mountains and through redwood forests, the ramshackle cottage, the vines and weeds, the immense task of fixing so much before she'd have a home again.

Slowly, Christy undressed, shedding pieces of clothing one by one and bit by bit, like peeling off a skin that was no longer her own. She pulled a nightgown from her overnight bag and pulled it over her head, then crawled into the narrow bed.

Maybe the bed was narrow. But when she pulled the covers up to her chin, they were soft and warm like the down of a gosling and hugged her tight. The fire outside faded into the rich velvet of a ripe summer plum, and then the moon rose, its silver light shimmering on the bed. Christy's breath became deep, and still, and calm like the ocean outside. The last thing she knew was that her new neighbor would show her how to garden, and that she liked pistachios very much, and that on the other side of the wall, her old friend was humming a sweet melody, and that the sea softly sang of grace and hope and healing.

CHAPTER 3

I'm glad Agatha was willing to share you so soon, Christy. I was worried that she'd keep you all to herself for a few weeks." Barbara's smile deepened the fine, dry lines in her cheeks. The immaculate, dusty-blue cashmere two-piece she wore was the perfect fit for the grand sitting room with its gorgeous chintz tapestries, towering floor vases, and precious antiques. To finish the effect, golden sunlight filtered through sheer gossamer curtains onto the cross-hatched parquet floor, casting a warm glow on the porcelain teacups and delicate tea set on the rosewood sofa table.

"What are you talking about, Barb?" Agatha bit into her slice of quiche lorraine. "Why would I keep her away from you?"

Christy smiled at her elegant hostess. "And I'm glad you invited me over so soon."

They'd seen each other plenty of times before Christy's half-year hiatus, but not since. It was nice to know that Barbara was eager to renew the friendship even though she had no doubt read all the bad press about Christy.

"I mean, I'd have brought her over for breakfast, but she slept until noon, and I didn't want to wake her since she obviously needed it," Agatha mumbled, her mouth full of buttery crust, ham, and cheese. "Barb's been feeling a little lonely. Or...what was it you said on the phone?"

"I said I was feeling a little *unsettled*. It's probably the wind. I always feel unsettled when it blows from the south." Even though Barbara was surely in her seventies, the light in her gray eyes was that of a twenty-year-old when she turned back to Christy. "Would you like another cup of tea, my dear?"

"I've had plenty, thank you. Everything's delicious, Barbara." Christy wished again the cat hair would have come off her suit. It was all right in Agatha's cottage. But here, where everything screamed of the understated luxury of true wealth, she felt uncomfortably shabby.

"I'll have another one of those little cuties," Agatha declared staunchly and fished the last cucumber sandwich from the tiered silver tray. "They sure go down easy."

"Yes, they certainly do. Lukas, do you mind?" Barbara glanced at her butler. Nodding an almost imperceptible nod, he disappeared to return a minute later with a new silver tray full of delicacies. Soundlessly, he swapped it for the one Agatha had just emptied.

"Oh, you shouldn't have," Agatha said gleefully and took one more sandwich, opening it to study the inside. "What's this then? Pâté? Yummy."

"Foie gras, my dear. Imported from France, I believe, but I would have to ask Margrit." Folding her hands on her lap, Barbara leaned confidentially toward Christy. "Margrit is my cook. I'm beyond blessed to have her. Securing excellent help is a talent I inherited from my mother. Though I have to admit that she was even better than me. You wouldn't believe how her staff adored her. I sometimes think that there is nothing they wouldn't have done for her." She folded her hands and half looked over her shoulder. "Do you adore me, Lukas?"

A smile tugged on the butler's lips. "Of course, ma'am."

Barbara nodded contentedly. "I adore you too, Lukas. Anyways. How do you feel, Christy?"

Before Christy could think, an involuntary sigh escaped her lips.

Barbara nodded. "It can't be easy to give up the apartment you lived in for so long. Or deal with the shocking fallout from the forgery." She shook her head, her short white curls swaying. "I read everything about the case I could get my hands on. It goes without saying that I'm convinced you were not at fault, my dear."

"That's kind of you to say." Christy lowered her teacup. "But I should have spotted the signs. It cost the auction house a lot of money and embarrassment."

"Let's not worry very much about a multi-million corporation. Their stock is doing just fine; I checked on that too. In fact, I'm convinced their PR department quite enjoys a good scandal," Barbara assured her. "I want to know how you are, now that the storm has blown over. What's the fallout?"

"I'll never be asked to do a consultation again, that's for sure." Christy sat her cup on the saucer, the rose-petal porcelain clinking delicately. "What's worse, I seem to have lost a lot of friends over it."

"They were not your friends," Barbara's voice was gentle yet firm. "They were colleagues and business partners. Friends are the ones who are there for you not despite, but *because* this happened."

"*I*'m a friend." Agatha nodded at Christy. "I don't care if you miss a hundred forgeries."

"Neither do I," declared Barbara. "Count me as a friend too."

"Thank you," Christy murmured, suddenly blushing warmly. She had not spent enough time with Barbara to earn her friendship, and she'd frequently neglected Agatha for months at a time.

"Now." Barbara glanced over to see if Agatha had finished her food. "Let's take a little walk, ladies. I want to show you my new painting." She rose, straightening her cardigan.

"You paint?" Christy folded her snowy white linen napkin and put it beside her plate as she and Agatha stood as well.

"Do I paint? No. I *buy*." Barbara winked. "Aside from hiring the right people I can't really do anything well at all, and I have not a single artistic talent. I can't even fold a napkin, and my mother tried very hard to teach me."

"Your talent is that you're nice," Agatha said and tossed her gray hair back. "You're generous. And you're very, *very* good at being rich. You are the only person in Mendocino county who serves cucumber sandwiches on silver platters. Without the crust too." She nodded her appreciation at the butler, who nodded back stoically.

"Thank you kindly." Barbara laughed. "One does what one can. Follow me, ladies." She led the way out of the magnificent hall, turning into a long corridor. Large windows lit up the paintings hanging tall and heavy on the opposite wall. "Look at these." She stopped in front of one of the portraits. "I want your professional opinion if you'd be so kind, Christy."

Christy stepped in front of the large oil painting and studied the young woman who was depicted. Skillful brushstrokes traced her contours, bringing to life intelligent eyes and determined lips, a chin that knew how to be stubborn. The lines emphasized the woman's resilience and—grief? No, not grief exactly. Was it loneliness?

Christy tilted her head and frowned because there was a mystery here, something the woman kept to herself. Christy shifted her attention to the background.

Warm, comforting colors evoked the glow of a Mendocino sunset, with an atmosphere of nostalgia settling over a lush garden setting. In the background, the sea rolled and crashed against cliffs, her force clashing with the rich yellow roses and white camellias that grew all around the young woman.

"Is this your mother?" Christy asked. "I see a resemblance."

"It is my mother." Satisfied, Barbara nodded. "Her name was Ella. Ella Baker, née Meinhardt."

"Who made it?" Christy was rarely swayed by paintings. But this one, even though it wasn't as good as many others she'd seen, made her want to reach out and touch the woman's hand. No—she wanted to reach out and take the entire woman. Lift her out of that cage of camellias and roses that was trapping her, turn her around so she could see the danger that the stormy sea posed. *Never turn your back to the ocean, Christy*, her mother's words echoed through her head. *You never know what it's up to. Always watch the waves.*

"A local artist," Barbara said. "What do you two think of it?"

"I like it," Agatha said. "I think you showed me a photo like this once. Well, of the woman. The background is made up, isn't it?"

"Yes, you're right. I always liked how she looked in that photo, so I thought I'd want to have it as a painting." Barbary turned to Christy. "What do you say?"

Christy gave her a quick smile. "The execution is not perfect," she murmured. "But it is touching. It makes you feel something. In the end, that is what counts when it comes to art. The most technically perfect painting is worthless if it doesn't make the viewer feel." She nodded. "Your local artist did well. Keep an eye on him."

"Her," Barbara corrected, and she took a breath to say something more when Christy interrupted her.

"What happened to your mother?"

Barbara's mouth closed. Surprised, she looked over. "What do you mean?"

Afraid she'd put her foot in her mouth, Christy shook her head. "I'm sorry. I meant nothing."

"The woman looks sad," Agatha suddenly said. "Your mother looks sad, and she is trapped, even if it's in a cage made of beautiful flowers. Is that what you meant, Christy?"

Christy nodded. Agatha could be eccentric, but she was also perceptive and smart as a whip. "Yes, I suppose so. She does look weary."

For a while, Barbara did not speak. Then she said, "The photo was taken a short while after her only sister drowned in the sea. My aunt Doris. She was young. Much too young to die." She cleared her throat quietly. "My mother and Doris were close. They came from a strict family, you know, and their shared experiences bonded them." She tilted her head, looking at her mother's eyes. "Doris took care of my mother when she was pregnant with me. Unfortunately, I made as much trouble as I could and confined Mother to the house, if not the bed, for months. It was a difficult pregnancy for the times." Barbara sighed. "Yes, they were very close. Mother never got over losing her."

"Nobody gets over the loss of a sister," Agatha remarked softly. "Just thinking about it makes me glad I don't have one in the first place."

"It shows in her eyes," Christy murmured. "Was she in her garden when it happened?"

"Yes." Barbara's eyebrows rose. "I knew you were good with paintings, but my word. Yes, my mother was planting roses in the garden when it happened." For the first time, the corners of Barbara's mouth dropped. "A local woman who was collecting shells saw Doris go down. She said a rip tide caught her. My aunt's body was never recovered, which makes it likely that the current took her." She cleared her throat. "I don't like thinking about my aunt's death. It conjures up the terror of the time, my mother's grief, the fears that followed me for many years."

"Brrr." Agatha closed her eyes and shook, shivering at the short, sorry story. "I wish she hadn't gone swimming. The water is much too cold and dangerous around here."

"It is." Once again, the mild smile that seemed natural to Barbara's lips returned. "But she did go swimming every day, poor girl. I was never allowed to go into the water beyond ankle-deep. It's the way the sins of our forefathers come back to haunt us."

"Amen," Christy murmured. "Do you also have a painting of your aunt?"

Barbara shook her head. "Unfortunately, I don't. Look." She gestured at all the portraits hanging on the long wall. "Not another person under thirty in the lot."

"I think you should get yourself painted," Agatha remarked, squinting at the oils. "I always meant to ask why there isn't one of you."

Barbara lifted a teaching finger. "Because there's not a person alive among these portraits. I don't mean to join these ranks quite yet."

"Aha. Yes, don't do it," Agatha agreed and unceremoniously hooked her arm under Barbara's. "Come on, let's show Christy the rose garden."

"The same roses that are on the painting?" Christy gave the oil a last glance. The woman's smile, as mellow and enigmatic as that of the Mona Lisa, seemed to follow her.

"Yes, as a matter of fact," Barbara said. "Or so the gardener tells me. I have the opposite of a green thumb. The farther I stay away from my plants, the greener they get. But yes, he claims my mother planted most of them."

"And afterward, I think we should have an early dinner in the garden," Agatha said, opening the door at the end of the corridor. "Your butler looked like he had something good in the oven."

"Pork chops, I think," Barbara said. "Or carp in butter sauce."

"Carp? Who in the world eats carp? They taste terrible. I'd rather drink muddy water," Agatha complained, and then the door to the corridor with the portraits fell shut behind them with a heavy thud, and they went down a flight of sweeping stairs that led to the garden.

"I do. I have a pond where they live, and they happen to be quite tasty," Barbara countered and opened the door to the garden. Just then, a gust of wind swept in from the sea, tangling her hair and making her close her eyes.

"Are you okay?" Agatha asked, putting a hand on Barbara's arm. "Where does this wind come from all of a sudden?"

Barbara blinked and smoothed her hair back. "The wind is like that down here," she said. "Lukas explained it to me once, but I forgot again. Something something eddies." She shivered and rubbed her arms, even though she was wearing at least two-ply cashmere.

"Are you cold? We can go back inside," Agatha offered.

"No, I'm not cold." Barbara dropped her hands. "I feel unsettled again. As if something is going to happen soon."

"Maybe it's because we're here," Christy tried to joke. But her voice didn't sound right. She felt unsettled too. Not because of the wind or eddies, but because of her life. Maybe Barbara was picking up on the chaotic, restless energy that surrounded Christy like a cloud wherever she went.

"No, it's not you. I'm glad you came." Barbara put her hand on Christy's. A sapphire ring the size of a robin's egg on her hand sparkled as the sunlight hit, shooting a ray of blue light toward the water. "By the way, my dear, how much work does the cottage need?" She let go, walking out into the garden. It was full of blooming bushes and flowers. Boxwoods, rhododendrons, and laurels took turns with radiant roses and impossibly perfect camellias.

"A lot," Christy said. Pulling Agatha along, she followed. "I don't know the extent yet. I'll have to make a list of everything that needs to be done."

"I know good people." Barbara picked a white rose. "Let me know if you need names and numbers."

"Thank you," Christy said. "I will." Agatha asked who Barbara used, and Barbara asked the gardener's opinion on the new lawnmower, and soon, Christy forgot all about the sad eyes and mysterious smile she had seen on the painting in the old mansion.

CHAPTER 4

"At least we'll have food." With a sigh of relief, Agatha dropped the heavy picnic basket that was digging into her palm. With a satisfying *whop*, it landed on the wooden stair leading to Christy's cottage. A piece of rotted wood broke off the corner and tumbled onto the path.

Agatha pushed it aside with the tip of her sneaker. "Oh well," she said bracingly, aware that Christy didn't need another reminder of how much work the cottage needed. "I suppose the stairs need to be redone anyway. You don't want to step on wormy wood."

"I certainly don't." Christy looked like she was sick. "Ugh, Agatha. Where do I even begin?"

Agatha clapped her hands. "At the beginning," she recommended. "Let's have a look inside, shall we?"

"Yes. Let's see what the real damage is." Christy pulled the key from her cottage and tried to push it into the lock. "Of course it's rusty. Give me a minute." Muttering under her breath, Christy wiggled and shoved, trying to scrape off the rust and get the key to fit.

Certain that Christy was too busy to turn around, Agatha dropped her smile.

She had never seen Christy like this before. Even if they hadn't visited often, they'd known each other for many, many years. Christy had always been collected, impeccably elegant, and poised. But not now. Now, she was...frazzled. Exhausted. Her life, everything that seemed important to Christy, had disintegrated in front of her eyes. It had changed her personality.

At night, Agatha could hear her mumble in her sleep through the wall. Not words; it wasn't loud enough to make out those, and they probably wouldn't make sense anyway. But the dark shadows under Christy's eyes spoke loud enough of the bad dreams that disturbed her sleep. And for the first time ever, she was not dressed to the nines in heels and suits. Instead, she wore pleated corduroy pants and a T-shirt. It had never entered Agatha's head that her friend owned anything as lowbrow as a T-shirt.

"There we go." With a crack like that of a cookie breaking in half, the key turned. Cautiously, Christy pushed the cottage's front door open. "Okay. We're in." She turned around to smile at Agatha.

Agatha hurried to smile back. "Great. Let's check it out."

Christy took an audible breath, big enough to dive into the sea to gather abalone, and stepped inside.

Agatha followed a close second, leaving behind the bright sun of a gorgeous morning as she stepped over the creaking threshold into her neighbor's new home.

Silently, they looked around. A musty scent wafted through the air, mingling with the tang of salt from the sea. Sunlight filtered through cracked shutters, casting long shadows that danced upon the worn wooden floors. The walls, once painted white or maybe the yellow of lemon sugar, now bore the gray streaks and shadowy marks of time and neglect.

"Oy weh," Agatha said. "We've got our work cut out for us, don't we?"

"Yes," Christy murmured. She put one hand on her hip and one on her forehead, as if she was feeling a fever. "But it's not moldy, and it's not wet. I was so worried it would be. This, I can do. It's possible."

"It's definitely possible," Agatha promised. When she'd first moved into her cottage, it had also been in a state. Not quite *this* state...but definitely a state. "Well, what do you say?"

"I say there is a certain melancholic reverie to the place," Christy murmured. She turned to her, and Agatha was relieved to see a small smile. "I think it could be really nice," Christy said. "It needs cleaning and varnish and air and gauzy curtains and furniture in cheerful colors."

"Yes!" Agatha nodded eagerly. That was the spirit. Squaring her shoulders, she went to explore. "The floor is solid." She stamped experimentally on the wide floorboards. A few spots creaked in protest, but it was no worse than the floor in her own cottage. "Nice and solid. Nothing vibrates," she reported, satisfied they wouldn't become the victims of a cave-in.

"Let's get rid of this dust and air everything out." Christy went to the windows, and after several attempts to turn rusted handles, the glass panes and shutters opened wide. A gust of fresh air blew inside like a curious spring sprite, bringing with it the sweet scent of blooming roses and the warm fragrance of sun-warmed stones and lavender.

Standing in the open window, Christy took a deep breath. "Hmm."

"Good morning!" a young male voice rang out. "Anyone here?"

Agatha went to join her friend by the window. "Hello?" she yelled, louder than she had meant to. "Hello?"

"Hello! Agatha? It's River. Hazel is with me. Where are you?"

River and Hazel! The young doctor and the owner of a wedding dress boutique were two of Agatha's favorite young people in the cove. Even Christy had met them before.

Smiling, Christy also leaned out of the window. "We're inside! Come on in."

"There, the door stands open," they heard Hazel's higher voice. A second later, the young woman's footsteps clattered up the wooden stairs, and the couple appeared in the door.

"What a cute place!" Hazel exclaimed as she came to them. "Good morning, Agatha." She leaned forward and kissed Agatha's cheek.

"Hello, darling." Agatha fondly took Hazel's hand in her own and looked her up and down. The pretty dressmaker had always been stylish. But now that she and the young doctor were getting quite serious, she looked happy. There was a light in her eyes that had not been there before, and she had gained weight. The extra pounds looked good on her, giving her a radiance that hadn't been there before. "You look very well."

"I'm getting fat." Hazel pulled her hands to her waist and laughed. "Hello, Christy."

"It's good to see you," Christy said. "Did you happen to drive by and see our cars outside the house?"

"No." River joined them, holding out his hand to shake first Agatha's, then Christy's. "Mom said that you were here, so we came over."

"River is Jenny's son," Agatha said, in case Christy had forgotten.

"Yes of course, I remember. We met at the hotel at Beach and Forgotten, and then again at your mother's wedding."

"We even danced together," River said and smiled.

"So we did." The smile that spread over Christy's lips was genuine.

Agatha could understand why Hazel was so smitten with her young man. Nobody would be surprised if one of these days, a big old diamond ring appeared on the dressmaker's pretty fingers.

River took a breath. "Christy, my offer from last fall still stands. If there's anything we can do to help fix up the cottage, we're happy to do it."

"Oh." Christy blinked. "That's really kind of you, but..."

"But that's *very* kind of you," Agatha fell into her friend's words, glaring a warning not to reject the offer.

Christy had helped out Jenny with a bunch of valuable heirlooms last year.

Christy narrowed her eyes but didn't reply.

"This is how it works in a small town," Agatha declared staunchly. "Don't go saying to these families you won't accept their help after *you* helped *them*. What sort of manners would that be?"

Christy looked taken aback. "I only meant—"

"Not very nice manners," Agatha answered her own question.

Hazel laughed and put a hand on Christy's arm. "We offer help because we want to," she said. "I absolutely adore the cottages down here."

Christy's face softened as she looked at the young woman. "Do you?"

"Very much." Hazel smiled, her cheeks dimpling. "I'm a seamstress. If you need anything sewn, I'm your girl." She reached out and touched the faded, plaid flannel curtains in front of the window. "I think maybe these need to be replaced."

Agatha smiled. The seamstress was as lovely as the doctor was charming. It would be nice if the two got on with it and had a lot of cute little babies. Agatha *loved* babies. So chubby and sweet and innocent...

"We could widen the windows down here." River was already knocking against the walls as if he wanted to tear them down right this moment.

"I would like more light," Christy said. "I should talk with someone and come up with a plan. Is there an architect in the cove?"

"Not in the cove," Hazel said after thinking it over. "But there's someone on Mendocino Island. He's retired, but I think he would help out a local."

"That's right," Agatha agreed. "I don't know why I didn't think of him earlier."

"Great." Christy straightened her shoulders as if she was forming a plan. "I would feel more confident widening the windows if I knew what is safe to do. I'd like to leave all the weight-bearing walls alone so they can properly bear the weight, if you know what I mean."

"Sure," Agatha said, glad that Christy seemed to have regained some of her old efficiency. "You should absolutely find out which ones are weight-bearing walls. And uh...two-by-fours. Where *they* are. And so on."

Christy raised a critical eyebrow at that, as if Agatha was trying to be cute, but in the end decided to ignore the two-by-fours. She turned to Hazel instead. "If you can give me a name or a number, I'll call. It doesn't hurt to ask, I suppose."

"His first name is Ethan. But I'd have to look up his last name and his number," Hazel said. "I can't remember off the top of my head."

"Would you do that for me?" Christy looked grateful. "I'd feel much better if I had a professional opinion."

"Yes, of course." Hazel smiled. "I'll be happy to. I'll text you."

River's phone pinged, and the corners of his mouth dropped in an apology. "That's the office. I need to take this." He turned away to answer the phone.

"He's a doctor," Agatha mouthed at Christy, who mouthed back, "I *know*."

Pushing the phone back in his pocket, River returned. "I'm afraid the windows will have to wait for another day," he said and glanced at Hazel. "Looks like a young mother isn't going to make it to the hospital in time. I'll have to hurry if I want to be there when the baby comes."

"Ooh, a baby? Who is it?" Quickly, Agatha ran through the names of all the pregnant women in the cove and the island. There weren't many, not nearly enough, but still a few. "Is it Megan?"

But River was already on his way out. Agatha couldn't tell whether he hadn't heard or didn't want to hear, but it didn't matter. The news would spread almost as quickly as the baby seemed to be coming.

"I'll text Agatha Ethan's number, since I don't have yours, Christy," Hazel said hastily, already hurrying after River. "I'll see you real soon."

"Thank you for stopping by," was all Christy had time to say, and Agatha yelled, "Good luck!" before they heard the tires of River's car screech on the street as he sped off.

The two women turned to face each other.

Agatha grinned. "I bet it's Megan. It's her third. The first baby takes its sweet time, the second baby makes trouble, and the third baby shoots out like nobody's business."

Christy shivered as if Agatha had said something gross. "You should become a midwife." She closed the window. "Let's go and look at the rest of the cottage."

Agatha sighed. "Let's go eat first. I'm starving."

The baby talk had reminded her of her only grandchild, little Ryan. Well, not so little anymore either. It was easy to forget now because his parents had moved away, to be closer to work and childcare. Unfortunately, it just wasn't practical for them to commute from their old place near Mendocino Cove.

Now that they couldn't visit so often anymore, Agatha was missing all the little strands that wove together Ryan's life. The few times they had spoken or chatted on the phone, he didn't try to catch her up. Or maybe he had tried. But Agatha didn't understand half the words and abbreviations he used, and there was never a good time to ask anymore.

If it were up to her, Agatha would gladly do the two-hour drive to see the young family. But...she simply couldn't show up at their doorstep every other day. They had enough to do without Grandma sitting around the living room and needing to be entertained or clogging up the kitchen. Their daily routine was a carefully crafted ballet that Agatha couldn't improve, only disturb.

At least that was Agatha's impression.

She'd often thought about selling her cottage and moving closer to her son. But when it came to bringing the idea up with him, she'd always balked. The last time they spoke, Bobby had said he didn't even know how long they would live there anymore. He might have to follow his job as a software engineer and move away. Like Silicon Valley. Or all the way across the world to Singapore.

Every time Agatha would see her grandchild, Ryan would be a little older, a little more distant, a little less interested in staying in touch.

But that was the way of the world. If the only thing she could do to help her son's family was to leave them be, then, she supposed, that was her job. It didn't come easy, but what about being a mother and a grandmother was easy?

"Let's get you out of this dusty cottage and into the fresh air." Christy put a hand on Agatha's shoulder, interrupting her thoughts. "A sandwich and a slice of that chocolate pistachio torte will do you good, my dear."

"Fine." Agatha swallowed her lonely thoughts. Nobody who had old friends and seaside cottages and cream tortes had a right to complain. "Fine. But then we'll finally explore the rest of the cottage."

CHAPTER 5

"What did you bring?" Christy sat on the sun-warmed stone step, facing an azure sea.

Agatha handed her a paper napkin. "Goodies." She was glad to be back under the bright blue sky. The inside of the cottage had felt gloomy, never mind that it had potential.

"Yes, but what goodies?" Christy asked, her voice mildly curious. She wasn't a big eater and was obviously trying to distract Agatha by giving her a chance to talk about cooking and baking.

Grateful nevertheless, Agatha smiled. Christy was lousy about staying in touch, and stubborn, and much too high-strung for her own good. But under all the glitz and glam, she was also kind. If Agatha were to lose her home, Christy would probably invite her to stay at her place too.

"I have sandwiches," Agatha said. "And lemonade made from the strawberries in my garden."

"What kind of sandwiches?" For the first time since she'd arrived, there was a new note in Christy's voice. Something nicer, something softer than before.

"Two kinds." Agatha pulled herself together, casting off thoughts of being unwanted by either her family or friends. "One is a brie and apple croissant." She pulled out two plastic containers and set them on the step. Paper bags would have crushed the flaky croissants that Billie had baked that morning and kindly brought over. "It has brie cheese, thinly sliced green apple, honey, walnuts, and uh...arugula from Billie's kitchen garden."

Christy's eyebrows rose. "That sounds nice. What's the other kind of sandwich?"

Agatha lifted another container from the crammed basket. "Just a simple caprese pesto ciabatta sandwich," she said. "Actually, Jon, Billie's brother, made them for us. Billie told him we'd be out at the cottage today, taking stock."

"Really?" Christy pressed her lips together. For once, she was not wearing her signature red lipstick. "He made us sandwiches?"

"Yes, he's always cooking for others, and so is Billie," Agatha said. "Isn't that nice? I think that's nice."

"I also think that's nice," Christy said. "I can't remember the last time someone made me a sandwich. At least not without me having to ask first. I kind of assumed that when my mother passed, it wouldn't happen again in this life."

Agatha glanced at her. Christy could be terribly capable if she wanted to be, but she didn't seem to have many people in the city who nurtured her—without her first having to ask. Agatha also didn't get sandwiches every day. But sometimes. Often enough.

"Well, we have these," she said and set the caprese sandwiches next to the brie croissants. "Made with fresh mozzarella, tomatoes, and basil—Jon grows the tomatoes and basil in the vineyard—his secret pesto sauce and balsamic glaze."

"I am very hungry," Christy said, sounding surprised. "Where do we start?"

"It doesn't matter." Agatha lifted two more containers out, which concluded their savory options. "Take whatever you like." She handed Christy a paper plate and plastic fork and opened the containers. "We also have lemon herb roasted chicken drumsticks and Mediterranean pasta salad with cherry tomatoes, olives, feta cheese, and cucumbers."

"Did Jon make these as well?" Christy inhaled the fresh scent of the salad's light vinaigrette and the citrusy scent of the roast chicken.

Agatha shook her head and put a juicy, crisp drumstick on her plate. "Actually, Faye dropped these off. Before breakfast, right after Billie and before Jon stopped by. You were still sleeping."

"Faye!" Christy liked the woman who ran a little store full of antique treasures. "How is she?"

"She's got a little girl now," Agatha reported. "Happily married to her detective and busy with the baby. Her name is Gabby, and she knows how to keep her mama on her toes."

"What was her husband's name again?" Christy helped herself to a caprese sandwich and the pasta salad.

"Gabe. That's why. Gabby and Gabe. Faye thought it was cute."

"It is cute," Christy said. "Don't you agree?"

"Yes," said Agatha. She bit into her drumstick, enjoying the combination of roasted garlic, pepper, and lemon. "I think it's cute. Especially when you see the proud father walking around with the baby in his arms, all pink and chubby cheeks. I mean, the baby wears pink and has chubby cheeks."

And just like that, Agatha felt better. Being an old woman without any family in town wasn't so bad. Christy poured them strawberry lemonade, and they sat in the sun of a beautiful, golden-blue day and drank it, tasting the delicious foods their friends had prepared for them and enjoying the warm, lavender-scented air on their faces.

"I don't think I can eat another bite after this one." Christy put the last of the sandwich in her mouth and chewed.

"All right." Agatha wiped her hands with a paper napkin and closed the containers. "Dessert."

"Dessert?" Christy shook her head. "I wish I could, but I can't. Uh—what is it?"

"Chocolate-dipped strawberries," Agatha announced. She'd specially kept them on ice so they would be nice and cool, the chocolate crispy to the bite. She liked when it splintered into her mouth, followed by the sweetness of the ripe berries. "At least try them. I have too many strawberries in the garden."

"That's not necessarily a bad thing." Christy covered her mouth with the tips of her fingers and hiccuped.

"And here are my special lemon tartlets. I've perfected the recipe, if I may say so. They are just so tangy and sweet and refreshing." Agatha pulled the containers from the basket and opened them. The fragrance filled the air, making her mouth water even though she had just eaten a sandwich as big as her hand. "I do like lemon a lot."

"Yes, you do. Mh-hmmm. I can smell them from here. Well, how can I resist? Since you're twisting my arm, I must sample them."

Delighted, Agatha held out the boxes, and her friend helped herself to both a strawberry and a sweet tart.

They ate in silence, enjoying the fruity-sweet combinations. Only the clear, fluting song of a late hermit thrush accompanied the gentle rushing of waves lapping at the sandy beach.

"This is so nice," Christy said suddenly. "Agatha, I feel better than I have in days. And I haven't even started renovating the cottage yet."

Agatha nodded. She folded up the legs of her jeans, letting the skin of her legs soak up the sun. "The cove is good for the nerves," she said. "You have had so much stress lately. It's time you get to enjoy yourself for a change. You deserve it."

"Do I?" Christy picked a sprig of lavender. "I made a bad mistake with the painting. I know mistakes happen to the best of us. But I deserved everything I had coming. I should have known better."

"That's the thing," Agatha said. "We all know better. That's why it's a mistake. Why should you think it's okay for others to make them but not give yourself the same grace?"

"I don't know." Christy smelled the lavender. "Perfectionism, I suppose. I always had to be perfect to get ahead."

"But Christy, that's all over now." Agatha turned her head to lazily blink at her friend. "We're retired. We don't have to be perfect anymore. Nobody expects anything of us." She turned back to the sea, chewing her lip. "At least not of me, other than that I take care of myself and don't be a burden."

Christy lowered her head, studying the lavender sprig she was holding. "You are right. It's very different from before."

"It is. But once you sit in your cottage and every day is the same, peaceful and full of sun and sea and the rushing of the waves...eventually you'll understand deep down that making a mistake here and there is okay."

"Let's drink to that. Here's to the sun and the sea and making mistakes." Christy lifted her glass full of iced strawberry lemonade.

Agatha clicked her own glass to it. "Cheers," she said and drank. Then she wiped her mouth and took a deep breath. "And now we go and have a look at the rest of the cottage. Can't be scared to do it."

"I can't be scared," Christy agreed and started putting the plates and containers back into the basket. "And I'm not. I'm just...spooked. By the change, and how fast it is happening."

"That, too, shall pass. Come on, let's explore your little cottage queendom and see what all needs to be done." Agatha held out a hand and easily tugged her skinny friend to her feet.

CHAPTER 6

A sudden gust of wind snarled through the air, carrying a rare chill in its wake. The morning had started out foggy and gray, the way it often did. But instead of drying up as usual, the air had only gotten soggier with every passing hour. While the moisture was probably good for the plants after two weeks of unbroken sunshine, Barbara never liked a rising wind.

The gust tugged on her open waxed jacket, pulling it here and there, unable to make up its mind. She hugged the flaps closed and turned to check on her friends, admitting to herself that it had been a mistake to come out for a walk. Behind her, her shoes had left deep impressions in the sand, the heels digging holes that quickly filled with foaming water.

Christy had it worst because she was wearing a pleated skirt. It was navy and elegant and very good quality indeed, but in this weather, the hem flipped and floundered, ready to embarrass its wearer at any moment.

Agatha, on the other hand, was not only wearing her most comfortable pair of jeans—at least Barbara imagined it was her most comfortable pair, worn and baggy as it was— but also rain boots and a flannel jacket.

Warm and protected, her only adversary seemed to be her hair. She had let it grow longer over the last year, and now the wiry gray and pepper strands twisted around her head like Medusa's snakes, angry and untamable. Frowning, Agatha reached up and swatted a wily strand of hair out of the way.

Barbara smiled and stopped to wait for them.

The beach usually spread like a golden rug before the park grounds. Whether the rug was rolled out to invite the sea to the house or the house to the sea, Barbara could never decide. But today it didn't matter, since it was far from being either golden or inviting. The sand was beige, still wet from tide and dew, looking more like a bandage than a welcome rug.

Always watch the ocean, her mother's voice echoed in her head. *Always, always watch the waves.*

Ducking against another salty gust, Barbara scanned the thrashing sea. They were walking high up on the strip of sand, much higher than she usually walked. Normally, the bleached skeletons of driftwood warmed their bones in the sun here. Shells that had lost their color to age and elements lay sprinkled around, and bits of dried kelp, as hard as thorns, nestled in the sand that the tide never washed clean.

But now, waves ran up the beach like white-crested tentacles, groping for the sea's long-forgotten possessions to return them to the ocean. Barbara sidestepped a foamy fringe and turned to her friends. "We should probably go back," she called into the wind.

"What?" Agatha squinted at her.

"Go back!" Barbara pointed at the house and raised her eyebrows. "Tea!"

"Good idea!" Christy slapped down her skirt with a now practiced gesture. "It's just too stormy to walk!"

Barbara nodded and started back. Despite the storm, it wasn't cold—they could sit in the winter garden while they had tea. That way, they'd still have light and plants and sky, but the wind wouldn't bother them.

It didn't take long to get to the winter garden. The wind, as if it wanted them gone, pushed against their backs, shortening the time it took to get home by half.

"Phooey!" Barbara closed the glass door behind Agatha. She took a deep breath of the calm, green air in the winter garden and smiled. "Grab a chair, you two. I'll get us something to eat."

Lukas appeared in the door to the hall, a small frown between his eyes. "I was waiting for you, ma'am," he said in a low voice and came over to help her out of her waxed jacket. "This is no weather for a walk so close to the sea."

"Well, we are back now." She smiled at Lukas. Her butler was only a year younger than her, but he was one of those mysteriously ageless men with timeless features. A long time ago, when Barbara had been looking for help in the large house and Lukas had been looking for a new position, a friend had recommended him.

From the first day, Lukas had made both Barbara's and her cook Margrit's lives easier. No, not easier—better. Life was better with him in the house. Secretly, Barbara waited for him and Margrit to fall in love. She liked the idea of giving them the guest cottage as a wedding present someday.

"We would like tea, if it's no trouble," she said.

Lukas took Agatha's jacket as well. "Margrit has already prepared it." A smile showed in his eyes as he said the cook's name. Before Barbara could ask for details on what they'd have for tea, he left.

"I think of all the things I envy in your life, Barb, having a butler takes the top spot." Agatha's words sounded heartfelt as she looked after him.

"Yes, I'm sure. But you'll have to come here to see Lukas." Barbara chuckled. "I can't spare him. Or Margrit. I can't do without either one."

"Well, that's as it should be. After all, I couldn't pay their salaries. And I enjoy making my own tea," Agatha concluded cheerfully. She plopped into one of the graceful wicker chairs that stood between potted ferns, palms, and orchids, and sighed happily. "It's much more pleasant to watch the sea from inside when it's stormy, isn't it?"

"Yes." Christy also took a chair. The rattan creaked when she sat down. Carefully, she smoothed her pleated skirt. "Such a beautiful room," she noted. "All glass and green arcs and plants. Do you spend a lot of time here?"

"As much as I can," Barbara said. "Though I also like the library on a rainy night. It has a fireplace, you know."

"Tell me about the house while we wait for the tea," Christy said.

Barbara smiled and sat as well, launching into the mansion's history. The seaside mansion outside of Mendocino Cove wasn't as old as it seemed but still historically significant. Her father had been the only heir of an old and famously wealthy family, sent out to conquer the newspaper business in the West.

Barbara had loved her larger-than-life father. She remembered him to be always loud, always in a good mood, with a booming laugh that filled the house from basement to attic. As the head of several large companies, his presence was in high demand. Luckily, traveling, board meetings, and sumptuous business dinners energized him. He was successful and enjoyed himself hugely in the process—and when the time came for Barbara to execute his will, she suspected he had also enjoyed several affairs with women.

Unlike her husband who had split his time between several homes and many hotels, his wife preferred to stay at the family seat. It was where she wanted to raise Barbara, and Barbara was grateful for it. She loved the rugged coast of Northern California, and even though she had traveled in her youth, she had always returned here.

"By the way," she said to Christy just as Lukas returned with the tea tray. "My family used to own the three cottages in Mendocino Cove."

"Really?" Christy looked surprised. "Was it your real estate agent I was dealing with?"

"No, we sold the cottages many years ago. One to Agatha's parents, one to the Donovan family. I believe Billie still lives there."

"Yes," Agatha replied and rose to check out the food. "Billie lives there, and I do, and obviously now Christy does too."

Barbara joined Agatha at the tea table. "I remember that the third cottage was bought by a single gentleman who lived there all by himself. I understood that he was an artist. He lived there until he died."

"That's probably why the cottage is in a bit of a state," Christy replied. "Honestly, I was worried when I first got here. But Agatha and I went inside just this morning, and it's not as bad as all that. We just made a list of everything that needs fixing."

"Yeah, it's definitely doable. Structurally, everything seems okay." Agatha turned to Lukas, who was entering the room with another fully laden silver tray. "Oh, what's this? Do we get something to drink other than tea for once?"

He lowered the tray so she could see. "Margrit sends champagne, or, if you prefer no alcohol, sparkling elderflower mocktails, white peony tea, and jasmine tea. It has hand-rolled jasmine-infused green tea pearls." He smiled. "They're Margrit's specialty, and I'd like to mention that they're a spectacular addition to a cup of tea."

"I've never even heard of tea pearls, but I'm sure they are very nice. I'll try them right after this." Agatha helped herself to a flute of champagne while Christy, who was driving, picked the mocktail.

"I thought I would treat us to a little celebratory tea since the weather is so foul," Barbara said. She was delighted that her guests seemed happily surprised by the lunch choices. She took the flute of champagne Lukas brought her and cheered her friends before sipping.

She didn't often entertain, but she enjoyed having the two friends over. Agatha could be a bit rugged at times, but Christy's class and elegance tempered the effect. Likewise, Christy could be a bit distant and distracted, but Agatha's warmth never left space for an awkward pause.

"What did Margrit make us?" she asked Lukas. "Not cucumber sandwiches, I see."

Lukas went to the table, pointing out the choices. "Smoked salmon canapés," he explained. "I believe it is thinly sliced smoked salmon on crisp, small toasts with herbed cream cheese and a touch of dill." He indicated another tray. "Tartlets filled with a blend of truffle-infused mushrooms on creamy cheese. And this is prosciutto-wrapped, roasted asparagus."

"Goodness," said Agatha. "Margrit went all out, didn't she?"

"She always does." Lukas smiled politely, but the expression in his eyes said that Agatha had seen nothing yet. "On the tiered tray over here are poppy seed scones, lavender macarons, and honey madeleines. There is also fresh clotted cream and zesty lemon curd to go with the scones."

Christy smiled. "Madeleines are my favorite."

"Thank you, Lukas," Barbara said. "Tell Margrit everything smells and looks absolutely delicious."

"Thank you, ma'am. I will. I'm sure she'll be glad to hear it." He left to report to Margrit—who no doubt was already waiting for him—how her food had been received.

Barbara smiled. "Help yourselves," she said, and they all filled their plates with delicacies and ate while the wind whipped the sea foamy and whirled around the winter garden, knocking on the glass and rattling the green metal arches that held it.

"Do you know more about the man who used to own the third cottage?" Christy asked eventually and got up to pour herself a cup of the steaming peony tea.

"Not much, I'm afraid." Barbara dabbed the corners of her mouth with a napkin. "His name was Jimmy, I believe. I always thought of him as a bit of a hermit."

"Same," Agatha agreed. "I remember him sitting on the beach for hours when I was a child, looking out at the sea."

Barbara nodded; she had heard stories like that as well. "I think I liked him," she said. "But my mother, Ella, asked me not to talk to him." She shrugged. "I don't know why. Maybe she wanted to keep me away out of an abundance of caution. I don't know. But we didn't go to Mendocino Cove very often, and when we did, it wasn't usually to visit anyone anyway. Least of all single men."

"Your mother didn't ask you not to talk to *us*," Agatha remarked. "Nor the Donovans."

"You weren't a single man. And it's impossible not to talk to the Donovans when you're in Mendocino Cove." Barbara smiled. "They are everywhere, aren't they? But you are right. My mother never asked me to stay away from any of the other local families." She held out her teacup, and Christy refilled it. "Maybe she was angry he bought that particular cottage. I remember that my mother really wanted to keep it. It was the closest she ever came to an argument with my father."

"Why? What's special about this cottage?" Looking alarmed, Christy set her honey madeleine back on her plate.

Barbara sighed. "My mother's sister, Doris, lived in that cottage for a few years. I think after she drowned, my mother wanted to keep the place just as it was, so she had a place to go and remember Doris. I'm speculating, though. I was only four. It was a long, long time ago."

"If it had been my sister, I'd have wanted to keep the cottage too," Christy said. "It must have been difficult for your mother to give it up."

"My mother always gave in to my father. It's possible he never quite realized how much she loved and missed Doris." Barbara sipped her tea. She didn't want to weigh down her guests anymore with talk about lost sisters and family tragedies. Especially on a stormy day like this, when the sea was greedy, gnawing on the land like a hungry beast. She cleared her throat. "Who wants another scone?"

"Me." Agatha took one and helped herself to the last of the clotted cream.

"Have I told the story of the emerald phoenix brooch yet?" Maybe sensing her host's wishes, Christy launched into a story about a precious art object that had been stolen and recovered through a series of outrageous hijinks.

Barbara smiled and crumbled her scone to bits between her fingertips and followed her own thoughts.

It really was an awfully long time ago. But Barbara still remembered her lovely, beautiful, warm, young aunt. Barbara still missed her, like a favorite scent she couldn't quite remember, a tune she'd loved and forgotten, a word that lived on the tip of her tongue and was never spoken.

Barbara looked out at the stormy sea.

All these years later, she still missed Doris.

CHAPTER 7

E than is coming over today," Agatha remarked and bit into a breakfast bagel smeared thick with cream cheese and honey.

Christy glanced across the patio table at her friend while pouring herself another cup of strong, black coffee. The coffee, made from fresh well water and the heavenly scented roasted beans Agatha ground by hand in her little coffee mill every morning, was piping hot. She didn't know what it was about Mendocino Cove. Maybe the sea's lullaby, maybe the salty air, maybe the fact that she no longer carried her professional life on her shoulders.

But in the narrow bed in her friend's cottage, she could finally sleep. Her body was catching up on all the moonlight hours she'd lain awake over the last months. This morning, Agatha had barely been able to rouse her even though the storm had passed, and the light and sky of the new morning were as soft and blue and pink and sweet as newborn babies swaddled in plush blankets.

Christy sipped again from her heavy stoneware mug before she asked, "Who is Ethan again?"

"The architect," Agatha mumbled with a full mouth. "You said you wanted an architect to look at the house. Hazel sent me his number just like she promised, but I happened to stand in line behind him at the market yesterday and chatted him up. He said he could come over to take a look. But it needed to be today."

"Ah. *Architect* Ethan. Great, that's progress. Thank you for doing that, Agatha." Christy ate a forkful of scrambled eggs with dill shrimp. It melted, rich and savory, on the tongue. "When will he get here?"

Agatha checked her phone for the time. "In an hour or so. He'll go straight to your cottage."

"I'll be over there." Christy opened the jar of Agatha's homemade strawberry compote. In the salty seaside air, the compote smelled of summer and smiles and sun on bare arms. Christy inhaled deeply. "Mh-hmm. This scent can heal anything," she said, convinced it was true.

"Have it on this." Agatha pushed the breadbasket across the table and shooed away an interested gull who swooped in for a closer look. "It's sourdough bread. Jon brought it over when you were still asleep."

"Unbelievable." Christy slathered a thick, warm slice of the sourdough bread with the sweet-smelling jam and smiled at how pretty it looked.

"We're lucky to have Donovans around." Agatha picked up her newspaper and started reading. She was still in her morning robe, her hair unkempt and straggly.

Christy wasn't looking much better. She'd put on an oversized knit sweater over her pinstripe PJs but was barefoot and just as scraggly bed-haired as her friend. "Do they only bring us breakfast?" she asked after a while. The fresh bread was delicious, and so was the jam. Fresh, sun-ripened, earthy goodness.

Agatha glanced over the rim of her reading glasses. "They bring everyone breakfast. They always make too much so they can share with their neighbors. You'll see; they'll stop by your place too, once you move in."

"Sweet." Christy took another bite. She owned a small, charming, and quite valuable still life showing an overflowing breakfast table. It would make the perfect thank-you gift for the siblings.

"Are you going to start cleaning the cottage today?" Agatha put the paper down again, as if she'd decided to let the news be. "You can take the mop and the good squeegee."

"I will. Thank you." Already, Christy had eaten more than she should have. Her stomach felt full under the comfy sweater. "I think I'm gaining weight."

"Nobody ever got fat from fresh sourdough and homemade strawberry jam," Agatha said firmly. "The stress of your old life starved you. Now that you're relaxing into life here at the coast, your body is finally taking care of itself. Let it sleep. Let it eat. You'll live longer. You'll live *happier*."

"I'm astonished that I can eat this much." Christy popped the last bite into her mouth.

Smiling, Agatha raked her fingers through her white hair. "Then you like my food?"

Christy smiled back. "I *love* your food, dear friend. Thank you for making breakfast. By the way, is there a clothes store in town? I can't always walk around in tights and pencil skirts."

"There's one on the island," Agatha said. "You'll have to take the ferry. The son of the island's lighthouse keeper is the ferry's captain now. And, by the way, Billie is still dating the lighthouse keeper. I think it's getting pretty serious."

"Good to know. You should catch me up on all the local gossip."

"We'll grill salmon steaks out here tonight and have gin and tonics," Agatha decided. "It's going to be a warm night and a full moon. Perfect for bringing you up to speed on local lore."

"Lore?"

"Gossip, I mean. I know everything that's going on in this town."

Christy chuckled. "I bet you do." She set down her mug and pulled a foot up on her wooden chair. "I can't wait until the cottage is done, Agatha. We'll have a good time as neighbors, won't we?"

Agatha took her reading glasses off. "Do you think you'll miss your old job? Do you think you'll get bored?"

"Hmm." Christy had only been in Mendocino Cove for a few days. But the food, the sleep, and the no-pressure company of good friends had already made her feel much better. "Not for a while," she replied to Agatha's question. "Maybe in a while, when I've gotten used to watching waves and smelling lavender and walking on the beach. But who knows." She stood, checking the time so she wouldn't miss the architect Ethan. "A lot can happen between now and then."

"A lot can happen," Agatha agreed. "Go ahead and get ready. I'll have another cup of coffee on my own."

"I'll clean up when I get back. Don't you do a thing."

Agatha folded her hands behind her head and leaned back, closing her eyes and holding her face in the sun. "My kitchen, my rules," she said peacefully. "Go clean up your own cottage."

"Alright." Christy went upstairs to shower. There wasn't much incentive to stay longer than necessary in the tiny bathroom, so she decided to forego make-up in favor of sunscreen and be done. Her short hair would dry quickly in the sun.

Back in her room, she put on her only pair of capri pants and a light sweater, promising herself that if she managed to pry open the lock to the shed, she'd reward herself with a ferry trip to the island. She needed seaside clothes. A sun hat, and a light dress for hot days. Something fleecy for cool nights and mornings, more comfortable pants to clean in, and flip-flops or sandals that wouldn't fill up with sand on the beach.

When she was done dressing, she went downstairs and gathered Agatha's good squeegee and the cleaning supplies she'd bought at the local market. "I'm leaving," she called through the kitchen door that led to the patio.

"Finally," Agatha murmured. Her eyes were closed, and her face stretched to the sun, looking so peaceful and relaxed that Christy chuckled as she left.

Instead of taking her car, Christy walked to her cottage. It was only five minutes door to door, and she enjoyed the cawing of the gulls and the whispering of the sea breeze in the cypresses that shaded the road.

When she got to her property, she stopped, suddenly realizing that this was the first time she was here on her own. No Agatha, no Billie. Nobody but her and her new home.

Standing on the road, she tilted her head and took in the sweet picture of the old, overgrown cottage before the backdrop of the sparkling ocean. How had she ever thought the job was too big to tackle? How had she ever been disappointed that this was her house? "Stupid," she said out loud and laughed at herself. "So unbelievably stupid."

"Do you mean me?" a male voice asked.

"Ah!" Christy wheeled on her heel, dropping her bucket, gasping with surprise. Sponges, scrubbers, and rubber gloves spilled into the weeds.

"Oh!" The man held up his open palms to show he didn't mean any harm. "I startled you! I'm sorry. I thought you heard me coming. Here, let me get this." He kneeled and shoved the scattered cleaning supplies back into the bucket. "There you go." He rose and handed them to Christy. "I'm Ethan, by the way. I was supposed to meet someone at this cottage today. You wouldn't happen to be Agatha's friend, would you?"

Christy took the bucket. Her heart was still racing. She put a hand to it as if that could calm down the erratic beat. "I am. I think you're meeting with me." She straightened, and for the first time, she fully looked at the man in front of her.

He was about her own age, sun-kissed and robust, exuding the vitality of a life spent embracing the great outdoors. His hair was dark but richly threaded with silver, and a well-groomed beard added to his rugged charm. His eyes were a mesmerizing shade of cerulean blue, dark with a depth that seemed to hold the sea itself. Their magnetic warmth drew her in like a lighthouse draws a lost sailor on a moonlit night...

Christy blinked. "Ethan?"

"Christy!" Ethan opened his mouth as if he couldn't get enough air. "Christy Bellaire."

"Ethan Conway." Christy took a step back. How had she not recognized him right away? "What are *you* doing here?"

Ethan spread his hands and shook his head once. "I live here, Christy. I've lived in Mendocino for years."

"I had no idea," she said, still reeling. "I didn't know."

Ethan rubbed his neck, giving her that up-side-down look she still remembered so well. "So then, if I may...what are *you* doing here, Christy?"

Christy bit her lip. Then she sighed. She was old now. Everything that had happened between her and Ethan was a lifetime ago. She lifted the bucket into her arm, holding it like a shield between them. "I live here too, Ethan," she said and nodded at her sun-drenched, vine-covered cottage. "And this is my home."

CHAPTER 8

For a long while, an eternity really, Ethan just looked at her. Then his mouth widened into a smile, he shook his head, and finally, he chuckled. "Fancy meeting Christy Bellaire here."

Christy tilted her head. The look in his blue eyes used to make her smile too—until it didn't. "Speak for yourself." She lowered the heavy bucket again and swiped her hair out of her face. It reminded her that today, of all days, she'd skipped the makeup. Every wrinkle, every shadow and hollow was on display in all its aged glory.

"What do we do now?" he asked and pushed his hands into the pockets of his jeans.

"What do you mean?"

He shrugged, still smiling. "So, are you talking to me again?"

"It's been thirty years," Christy said, her voice sounding more reasonable than she felt. Because it still hurt. Not his betrayal. But the fallout of the entire thing.

"I know." His lips pressed into a line. "Well, since we are back on speaking terms, do you still need an architect? I don't want to—" He broke off.

"Mess me around?" Christy looked at her hands, and when she looked up again, the smile was gone from his eyes.

"I'll stay if you want me to." He pointed a thumb over his shoulder. "Or I can leave you alone."

Christy shaded her eyes. It was getting hot, and the sensitive skin of her neck, already red from the sun, was starting to burn. "Um. Well, the thing is...I do need an architect."

Ethan opened his hands. "I'm happy to help you out, but there are also other architects. Maybe not in Mendocino. But somewhere."

She hesitated. They were both older now. Old, really, on the far end of middle age. The damage was done; it didn't matter anymore. There was no longer a reason to keep holding a grudge. She moistened her lip. "It's all right for me if it is for you."

Ethan's throat moved as if he wanted to say something, but then he just nodded. "Sure. Shall we have a look at the cottage? I do have to be at the university in an hour."

"Yes. Um, thanks for coming over and doing this. I know you're doing me a fa—" Christy had stepped on the stone path that led through the weeds and immediately slipped on a leaf, only catching herself in the nick of time. "Oops." Quickly, she straightened her shirt. "Careful. I still need to clean this up."

"Let me carry the bucket." Before she could protest, Ethan took the bucket from her.

Christy wiped her hands on her capri pants. She could carry her bucket herself, of course, but... "Thanks." It wasn't worth making a fuss. If it had been any other man, she wouldn't think twice about accepting the common courtesy.

When she reached the door, she almost fumbled the key but managed to catch it and unlock the door before he could offer to do that for her too. "Come on in." She walked in and held it open for him.

"Nice little place." His presence filled the space to a disconcerting degree, and Christy walked farther into the hallway to create distance. "So what's the plan?" He followed her into the living room.

"Uh, basically, I'd like to know what I can and can't do." Hastily, she opened the window to air the stuffy room. She was getting too warm entirely. "I'd like to widen most of the windows and maybe even add a door to the yard."

"That should be doable." Scanning his surroundings critically, Ethan walked past her into the kitchen, knocking on walls here and there and studying the exposed wooden beams on the whitewashed ceiling. "Do you have the blueprints?"

Following him at a distance, Christy shook her head. "I don't know that there are any," she said. "The cottages are pretty old. But I can ask Barbara."

He looked at her. "Barbara?"

"Her family used to own the cottages. They sold them years and years ago, but if anyone has any blueprints, it'd probably be her."

He turned away, pulling a small gadget from his pocket and pointing it at the wall. "It'd be easier if we had them, but no worries if she doesn't. Tell me more about what you would like to do in here."

"I'd like a big window instead of that small one." She pointed. "With a big windowsill for potted plants."

The gadget beeped as he moved it across the wall. "Should be doable. This thing here tells me where the load-bearing studs are. Looks good." He tucked the tool away again and squatted to inspect the area where the wall met the floor. He ran his hand along it, then glanced all around the empty room. "No obvious cracks." He rose, brushing off his hands.

"Is it that easy?" Christy smiled.

"It's just a first glance." He put his head into his neck and stared at the ceiling. "What's upstairs?"

"Three small bedrooms and a big bathroom." She cleared her throat. Suddenly, she could barely remember what it looked like up there. "And there should be an attic since the roof is gabled."

"Can I have a look?" He pointed up.

"Sure." She led the way up the wooden staircase.

Upstairs, Ethan walked through the bedrooms, pacing out their size and now and then taking notes on his phone. "And the attic?"

"Feel free to have a look," Christy said. "There's a hatch, but I haven't found anything to pull it open."

"Hmm." Ethan went back into the smaller bedroom. The closet door creaked, and a moment later, he returned with a wooden stick that had a hook on it. He grinned. "I don't know why, but these things are always in the closet of the smallest bedroom."

Christy stepped aside so he could pull open the trap door. A long ladder fell down, and Ethan climbed up, disappearing in the dark. Christy craned her neck but couldn't see anything. Only the beam of his phone flash swept across the opening once in a while. "How is it?" she called out.

"All right," his voice came back. "Needs a bit of work on the roof. Some modern insulation and new shingles would make your life easier in the long run." He reappeared in the rectangle of the opening and climbed down the ladder, folding it back up and closing the hatch.

Christy breathed a sigh of relief that he was back. Whether it was because of the magnetic effect of his cerulean eyes or just the fact that he hadn't broken an arm and a leg in her attic, she didn't need to think about. "Bats?" she asked.

Ethan looked at her. His face had smudges of dust and grime on it, and there was a string of cobweb in his hair. Smiling, Christy pointed at it. "You have something in your hair."

"What? Spiders? Men's best friends." He raked his hands through his hair and then pulled on the short sleeve of his T-shirt to wipe his face.

Christy stood close enough to smell his scent. Just like that, memories flooded back to her. Sitting beside him in Art History 101. Walking hand in hand through the streets of Haight-Ashbury, she with flowers in her hair. Dancing through the night at the Avalon Ballroom, too happy to hide her feelings. Sitting in his dad's motorboat in the bay, his arms around her as he showed her how to reel in a fish. The fish—and the rod—got away. He let it go so he could turn her in his arms to face him. It'd been their first kiss.

Ethan cleared his throat. "You shouldn't have many problems here, Christy. If you want, I'll come back and do a proper inspection."

"Yes, please."

"In the meantime, maybe you can ask your friend Barbara for the blueprints. It'd be good to have them. Easier, you know."

"Right. I'll do that."

He looked at the ceiling. Not like he suspected another attic, but like he needed a moment. Then he glanced back at her. "Any other structures on the property?"

"There's a little shed," she said. His scent was beginning to overwhelm her with pictures and scenes and feelings of the past. She rubbed her temple to make the memories stop. "Here, come. I'll show you." Hastily, she turned and hurried down the stairs, taking the steps two at a time. As if she were twenty again, skipping down the steps of the university's art department. Not a retired art historian in her sixties.

By the time she heard him follow her, Christy was already outside in the overgrown garden.

"That's the shed, huh?" He went to the door, lifting the padlock. "Do you have the key?"

She shook her head. "I texted the real estate agent, but he hasn't answered yet. It's been six months since I bought the place, so I'm sure my business is no longer a top priority. He's probably forgotten who I am."

"Tell me his name. I'll give him a call to remind him." Ethan reached up and ran his fingers along the small wooden ledge over the door. "Until then, maybe this will do it." He opened his hand to show her a small key.

"I'll be darned." She smiled in surprise. "Here I thought it was impossible to get into the shed. I'm starting to think nothing's safe from you."

"I already know that's what you think." Smiling back, Ethan turned to unlock the door, leaving her to guess about his meaning. After a moment of pushing and twisting, the rusty lock clicked and crunched. Ethan unhooked it, and when he pulled on the faded white door, it creaked open. He took a look inside.

"Whoa," he said. "Come here, Christy. Have a look at this."

CHAPTER 9

The air inside the shed was thick with the musky scent of the past when Christy joined Ethan at the door. Sunlight filtered through a dusty window, casting a warm glow on the myriad of objects that were crammed into the tiny space.

Ethan held the door while Christy stepped into the shed. "The last owner of the house was an artist, just like Barbara remembered," she said. "He was an artist, and he left all his supplies here when he died. As if he thought someone would one day come for it."

"It's like a strange treasure trove." Ethan entered behind her, standing so close in the cramped space that Christy felt the warmth radiating off his body.

"What's all this?" she said busily and picked up a tool from a bench beside her. "A chisel. He was a sculptor. Oh, look at the wooden easel over there. He was both a sculptor and a painter." She squinted to read the writing on a tube of oil paint, wishing she'd brought her glasses. Soon, she gave up and started to walk around the small space.

Sculpting supplies of every shape and size spilled haphazardly from shelves, creating a colorful chaos of brushes, chisels, and clay. Paintings stacked four, five canvasses deep leaned against the walls.

Christy picked up the closest one and studied it. It was a vibrant seascape. Not high art, nothing she'd have come across at an auction house, but pretty and pleasing. She put it back, rifling through the other paintings the old artist had left behind. An enigmatic portrait, the cottage, another seascape, this one of a stormy sea. "Pretty," she murmured. "I wonder if he didn't have anyone to leave them to."

Ethan put back the small figurine of a face cut from soapstone he'd been looking at. "I'm sure he had someone. We should try and find them."

Christy picked up the statue he'd just put down. "She looks like Abby," she said before she could stop herself. Her eyes flew to Ethan, who was glancing back at her. "I'm sorry," she said and set the figure back. "Just something about the eyes." She was already turning away when she felt his hand touch her arm.

"Nothing happened between your sister and me," he said in a voice that was low and soft and reminded her of their time together—the long evenings they'd spent walking along the water arm in arm, the nights in his studio flat, their picnic lunches on the boardwalk.

"*Some*thing happened, Ethan." She'd seen them kiss. Maybe she'd been a naive small-town girl when she first met him. But being a late bloomer, she'd learned quickly. There had been nothing innocent about the kiss her boyfriend had shared with her sister.

"It was one kiss. The one you saw. Abby and I both had too much to drink, and I shouldn't have brought her home. But you know all that already."

"Yes, I do. Don't worry, I understand. I didn't back then, but I do now."

He tilted his head as if he wasn't sure she did understand. "I was the worst kind of idiot back then. I'm sorry for what I did, Christy. I know how much I hurt you, and I'm sorry I ruin—"

"Let's forget about all that," she interrupted him. "It was a different life, and we were different people."

There was a pause before he spoke again. "Different people?"

"We were so very young. But now we are old." Christy forced a smile. "Now we are old and wise, aren't we?"

She didn't want to think about the kiss. Or the way her baby love, her first love ever, had run much too deep in her veins and her heart and her soul. She had been naive enough to dream of wedding bells and babies the moment Ethan kissed her in that fishing boat. She had that wake-up call coming. She realized it soon after he had kissed Abby. But despite the realization, the pain had been sharp and raw like a dagger. Bleeding and hurt, she hadn't handled the situation. She hadn't handled it at all, and she lost much because of it.

Losing Ethan was not what she regretted. At first, yes. But not later. He wasn't the source of her secret tears over the years, nor the reason her hands trembled when she reached for her phone to read an unexpected text in the middle of the night, nor the reason she wrote a hundred long emails only to hit delete.

The relationship with Ethan wasn't the true casualty. It had been the relationship with her sister.

She and Abby had never truly healed the breach. And strangely, it hadn't been Christy who hadn't been able to overlook the sisterly betrayal over a boy, but her sister. She'd rejected all offers of peace. Maybe because it had taken Christy too long to reach out. Maybe Abby was angry that Ethan had tried to get back with Christy.

Eventually, Christy had accepted Abby's cold shoulder and mostly let her be. Clearly, her sister wasn't interested in their family. Abby didn't even come to their parents' funerals, sending flowers instead. Christy sent yearly Christmas letters and presents for her nieces' birthdays. The nieces sent back dutiful thank-you letters with little updates on their lives, each one breaking Christy's heart a bit more.

Christy had always meant to make it better. But before she found the needed opening in her sister's shield, Abby had died in a car crash. After the funeral, her husband took Lucy and Maya back to England, where his family lived. They moved a couple more times, once to France, once to Wales. Soon, Christy no longer had an address, or an email, or a phone number. The last shred of contact was severed.

"You're asking me whether we are old and wise?" Ethan's blue eyes studied her face, as if he was trying to find something. His chest rose in a silent sigh, as if what he was looking for no longer existed. "Maybe," he said and turned to leave the shed. "Maybe you are right. Now, we are old and wise."

CHAPTER 10

"Thank you, Lukas. Very kind of you." Barbara leaned on her butler's arm to get out of the car. Agatha and Christy had already gotten out on their own, stretching luxuriously in the warm shade of the redwood trees that surrounded them like the giants of a fairytale.

Barbara smiled at her enthusiastic young friends and pulled on the sun hat Lukas handed her.

"Margrit prepared backpacks with snacks and water." Lukas went to the trunk of the car and opened it. "There is also a bottle of sunscreen in there, mosquito spray, and a whistle." He lifted three small blue backpacks from the trunk. "I know you didn't ask to carry anything. But these are not heavy; would you please take them with you? We want you to be as comfortable as possible."

"Well, I want to be as comfortable as possible as well. Thank you." Barbara took one of them, and her friends followed her example. She smiled at Lukas, perfectly aware of whose idea the comfort packs had really been. "So what is the whistle for?"

Only Lukas's eyes returned her smile. "In case you get lost. Please don't get in a situation where you might need it."

"We weren't planning on it," Barbara replied mildly. "We'll stay on the path, and you'll pick us up at the other end of it. Isn't that right?"

"Yes, that's right." He looked over his shoulder as if he expected bears and pumas to charge from the bushes. "I'd rather go with you all together, but..." He tilted his head in question.

"No, you can't," Barbara declared. "If you did, we couldn't gossip because we'd feel judged, and besides, I have no intention of climbing back up the path. I need you to take the car to the end of the trail."

He nodded. "I'll wait at the beach then," he murmured and checked his Rolex. "An hour."

Barbara took a deep breath. "As long as it takes. There's a restaurant on the beach. All you have to do is have a nice meal and stretch out your legs." She patted his arm. "Bye! See you."

"The backpacks are not too heavy?" He reached out, testing the tension on the shoulder strap.

"They are fine," Barbara replied patiently. "Thanks very much. Bye-bye."

Lukas tipped his non-existent chauffeur's hat and left.

"Barb," Agatha said. "I think your butler is worried."

Christy slipped her arms through the straps of her own pack and smiled. "I even think he's a little more than worried for you, Barb."

"What are you insinuating?" she asked haughtily.

"I saw the look in his eyes. Pure, unadulterated longing."

"You are terribly wrong." Barbara archly raised an eyebrow. "He's desperately in love with Margrit, I'll have you know."

"Are you sure?"

"Sure I'm sure." Barbara waved the topic away.

"I understand. I'd be in love with Margrit too." Agatha opened her bag and pulled out a bag of salt-and-vinegar chips. "Though there's nothing wrong with you either, Barb."

"How generous of you."

Agatha ripped open a chips bag. "You can die happy, eating Margrit's food. I mean, one. Not you in particular, Barb."

"Thank you. I wasn't planning on dying at the dinner table quite yet."

Agatha popped a chip into her mouth. "These are my favorites."

As Margrit well knew. "Right. No seducing my cook, and no littering either," Barbara ordered and started walking. "And no dilly-dallying. We are here to exercise so we can live another day and eat another one of Margrit's excellent meals."

"I couldn't fit into my pinstripe skirt this morning." Christy joined Barbara, waving Agatha to keep up.

"You live in Mendocino Cove now." Agatha noisily licked the salt off her fingers. "You no longer need to fit into pinstripe skirts. Get yourself a flowy tie-dye with an elastic waist."

"The pinstripe is a very good skirt, and I like wearing it." Christy narrowed her eyes as if she didn't care to fit in with the tie-dye crowd.

"Ah, nonsense." Agatha had finished her chips and crumpled the empty bag into an outside mesh pocket of her backpack. "Invent a new you."

"No, Agatha, I will *not*—"

"Aren't the trees marvelous?" Barbara raised her arms over her head, holding them wide as if she could embrace all of nature. "Doesn't the air smell of fern and brook and wild sorrel?"

That stopped them bickering.

Christy closed her eyes to inhale deeply, and Agatha bent to pluck a stem of the lush, bright-green wood sorrel that carpeted the forest floor to either side of the path.

"I can walk here whenever I want now." Christy sounded surprised, as if the fact had only just sunk in. "I can come here every morning and every night if I want."

"The best time is the middle of the day," Agatha said and bit off the clover-leafed head of her sorrel. "The tree shade is nice and cool. The beach is the place to be on mornings and evenings."

They had not gotten far into the woods yet, but Christy stopped short. "I have my own beach," she said. "Guys. I have *a beach*."

Both Barbara and Agatha laughed. "Yes, you do indeed," Barbara said. "Isn't that the best?"

Christy's chin dimpled somewhere between tears and laughter. "That's the best," she said. "I thought I'd miss the city so much. But I haven't missed it yet. Not for one moment."

"You probably will, at some point," Bar said reasonably. "Once you settle in and get used to Mendocino Cove. Of course you can go visit whenever you like. A night or two in a nice hotel and a concert or author reading at night never hurt anyone."

"I have my own *beach*," Christy murmured again, softer now. She shook her head, and they all started walking again.

"I'm glad it's finally sinking in." Agatha brushed a hand over a majestic eagle fern frond. "I was getting worried cove living wasn't for you. I've never seen a person moping over a seaside cottage."

Both Christy and Barbara laughed at that. "I wasn't *moping*." Christy sighed. "Or maybe I was. I'm sorry, Agatha."

"You were a touch depressed when you arrived," Barbara said. "But you do seem to feel better."

"I didn't see it at first," Christy said. "But it was time for me to leave San Francisco. Life is so different here that I no longer worry about what happened in my old life." She stepped over a root as large as her arm, her eyes thoughtful. "No, I still care. I still wish I had spotted the forgery. But now it truly feels like a mistake, not a disaster."

"There you go," Agatha said contentedly. "Nothing like a move to the country to put things into perspective."

"You are right," Barbara said. "By the way, talking about moving...my lawyer did find an old blueprint of the cottage, Christy. It was buried somewhere deep in the real estate papers, and I'm sorry Jimmy never got it. It should have gone to him when he bought the house."

"That's great," Christy said. "I mean, that you found the blueprints. Ethan's looked at everything he can, but the prints will help answer a couple of open questions without having to bring in heavy machinery."

"Who is this Ethan, exactly?" Barbara asked. She'd learned not to press her own people and tradesmen on her friends because often, her friends couldn't afford their rates. That said, more than once she had called someone she had on retainer to secretly help out a friend. Architects were important. If Ethan turned out to be suspect at all, she'd send over her own team.

"He's an old acquaintance." Christy slowed to admire the bulbous flowers of the graceful fairy lanterns that grew near a patch of blooming woodland stars. "I looked him up on the internet too." She launched into the story of Ethan's career, telling them of awards and prestigious projects and received honors. It soon became clear that Christy had researched her old acquaintance thoroughly.

"Ethan's good people," Agatha agreed when Christy was finally done. "You hear things, you know."

"I'm sure you do." Barbara smiled. If anyone knew what was going on in this small town, it was Agatha. "So what did you hear about him?"

"Only good things. After he retired, he turned his garage into an art studio for the local kids."

"I didn't know that." Christy looked at her friend, her eyes full of interest.

Agatha nodded. "The families appreciate not having to drive their kids all the way to Maytown for art classes. Plus, Ethan's teaching them for free."

"That's nice of him," Christy said absentmindedly, wiping her forehead.

"You should stop by his place sometime," Agatha said eagerly. "He designed the house himself, and there are always kids drawing or painting or messing around with clay, and the parents often stay to watch and talk and drink tea. It was a bit of a local meeting place last time I went."

"You took art classes from him?" Barbara glanced at her friend.

"No, but I used to take my grandson Ryan when his family still lived nearby. I haven't been to Ethan's place in a long time. I have no reason to go there anymore." Agatha stopped beside the hollowed-out stump of a felled redwood and touched the ancient wood.

"Are you tired, Agatha?" Barbara asked gently. Suddenly, Agatha looked tired.

"Maybe. It's hot."

"Let's sit and eat. We're halfway there."

The circle of dry, sun-warmed wood was large enough to fit twenty people. The shady spots in its embrace were filled with delicate maidenhair ferns, while wild irises in blue and purple had claimed sun-dappled areas. They all climbed into the ring—easy enough, since time had gnawed wide gates into the wall of wood—and had each found a comfortable spot to sit.

"What do we get today?" Smiling, Christy unpacked her lunch bag, pulling out neat packages and a small bottle. "The label is handwritten. It says, 'Forest Mint Tea.' How adorable."

"I believe...yes." Barbara inspected her own lunch wrapped in wax paper. "Margrit labeled her food for us too." She picked the little note from the package and held it at arm's length to read. "She made us her honey-glazed salmon sandwiches. *Grilled filet with redwood honey and herb-infused cream cheese on artisanal bread.*"

"What's redwood honey?" Agatha had unwrapped her sandwich and bit into it. "Mh-hmm. So good. It literally melts in your mouth."

"I think the bees go into the forest and get whatever they can. Or maybe redwoods have flowers? I'd have to ask Margrit." Barbara tasted her own succulent sandwich. "Yummy."

"This is exactly what I mean." Christy chewed and swallowed. "I'm going on walks to stay fit and end up eating four times the calories I burn."

"But do you regret it?" Agatha looked over, interested.

"Goodness, no. This is too delicious for regrets."
Christy licked a drip of golden-red honey off her
finger.

Agatha pulled out another bag and handed the label to Barbara. "I can't read this without my glasses."

"It says..." Barbara held it as far as she could and
squinted. "Wild mushroom quiche with caramelized
onions and creamy goat cheese."

Agatha swallowed the last bite of the sandwich in
her mouth and bit into the flaky crust. "Mmm. Marry
me, Margrit." She flicked a crumb off her leg.

"I love that quiche too." Barbara picked up the last
two labels. "We have desserts too. What did she think
we're doing? It's barely an hour's walk."

"If you aren't grateful, I'd also be more than happy
to poach your cook away from you," Christy said
heartlessly. "The woman is a wonder."

"But what do the cards say?" Agatha insisted.

"Right. This one says marzipan shortbread cookies,
and the other, chocolate-dipped blueberries with
edible flowers." Barbara couldn't finish her salmon
sandwich, but she was curious about the edible flowers and unwrapped hers. "How pretty." Protected by
a silicone ramekin, a small waffle bowl was filled with
fresh chocolate berries. In between the juicy berries,
Margrit had tucked delicate sugar-glazed jasmine
flowers. Their pure white made the deep cocoa color
of the dipped blueberries even more appetizing.

"I'm saving my berries for later," Christy announced
and peeled back the paper from her marzipan short-

bread. "These smell so good. All buttery and"—she bit into one—"*so* soft. Listen, Barb."

"Yes?"

"I was just joking before...but if you ever decide to downsize, I'll be happy to offer Margrit a position."

"Yes, I'll let her know." Barbara laughed. "But don't hold your breath. She has lifetime use of the dowager house. Besides, I still believe she's in love with Lukas."

"That makes it hard to make an offer she can't refuse." Christy smiled. "I suppose the smaller guest room and my company won't cut it."

"First, you have to make yourself an offer you can't refuse and fix up your cottage so you have a place to stay," Agatha remarked and leaned against the sun-soaked wood behind her. "I'd love to eat more. But I'm full."

"You'll take the rest home, won't you? I can't come back like this." Barbara put her unopened lunch items back into her backpack and drained her bottle of iced mint tea. "Ready to go on?"

Soon, they were back on the path, continuing their way through the enchanted, mysterious forest.

CHAPTER 11

Properly refreshed, they soon reached the end of the trail at the bottom of the mountain. Across the street, in a small beach parking lot, Barbara spotted her car. "Lukas is already waiting for us."

"I bet he is," Christy hummed beside her, but Barbara didn't deign to reply. Looking left and right, they crossed the street.

Lukas was sitting at one of the bistro tables with an empty plate before him. When he spotted them, he rose. "How was the walk?" He lifted the backpack off Barbara's shoulders, then helped her friends. "It's a little warm today. I ordered iced lemonade for you when I saw you come down the hill. It should be here any second."

"Lovely." Barbara brushed her hair back. "Any news?"

"The cottage blueprints you asked for came in while you were walking." Lukas put the backpacks on an empty chair at his table and pulled out the chairs at the next. "Would you care to sit and rest? I could get the blueprints for you and be back before you have finished."

"Yes please, Lukas, if you don't mind. That way, Christy can take them to her architect today." They sat, the lemonade arrived, and they all drank thirstily. It was even warmer here on the sunny beach than in the forest uphill where they'd started.

"Agatha?" a woman asked from the next table, and they turned to see Jenny smile at them.

"All three of you! How nice to see you. Christy, Barbara."

They greeted their young friend, and Christy said, "Hello, Jenny. Do you have a baby now?"

Jenny laughed, and Barbara smiled. Jenny was a local historian going on fifty, and they all knew the baby Jenny held was Gabby, her friend Faye's daughter. While Faye was younger than Jenny, the pregnancy had been a true surprise.

"She's adorable," Barbara said. She was very fond of kids. But never having had any herself, she tended to avoid babies. They were so terribly cute with their eyes and their cheeks and their little sounds, but highly unpredictable. One never knew when they would start crying. And Barbara never knew what to do to calm them down again, either. She'd finally decided that she had no talent for babies and gladly left them in more capable arms.

"Hello there." Faye was coming from inside the restaurant, closing her purse as if she'd just freshened up. "The whole gang! What brings you all over here?" She picked up Gabby and wiggled her, which made the baby laugh.

"We took a walk," Christy explained. "How are you? I haven't seen you since you had the baby."

"Very well, thanks." Faye smiled. "Maybe busier than I'd like, but I'm grateful to have people to fall back on. And yourself? I hear things were pretty hectic in San Francisco at the end."

"Yes." Christy cleared her throat. But Barbara thought that she didn't seem to mind talking about it so much anymore. She even managed a smile. "Yes, it was very stressful. I'm sure you've heard the stories."

"Don't be so sure." Faye sat down, the baby in her arms. "I'm too busy to listen to gossip."

"That might be for the best," Christy said. "I've only been here a few days, and it already seems to have happened in the past. Maybe that's where the whole thing should stay."

"Can I hold her for a moment, Faye?" Agatha suddenly asked. "Just for a moment? I promise I won't keep her long."

"Of course you can. Thank you, in fact. My arms are getting tired." Faye rose and went over to where Agatha was sitting, laying the baby in her arms. "She's figured out how to suddenly arch her back and flop like a fish. Make sure to hold on tight."

"Ryan did that all the time when he was little," Agatha said, losing herself in the baby's wide-eyed gaze.

Barbara and Christy smiled at each other. But Barbara also felt a sting in her heart for her friend. Agatha loved her family very much, but it wasn't practical for them to visit the cove often. The great loneliness of women whose family had left them behind was settling on her. Barbara's smile dried up. If only she could help.

"How is Ryan?" Faye asked as if her thoughts had gone the same route as Barbara's. "You said he was going to get another bunny—did that happen?"

Agatha took a breath, then exhaled. "You know what? I'm not sure. I haven't seen the kid in weeks. I'll call him tonight, unless..." Her lips moved silently as if she were counting. "No, he has soccer tonight. Maybe tomorrow."

"It's too bad they had to move," Faye said. "But I understand. I'd love to have Gabby in a tumble class. I need to socialize her somehow, but I don't know any other families with babies. There isn't even a playground in town." She turned to Jenny. "Where's the closest playground? Do you know?"

Jenny shook her head. "Only the one in Maytown I told you about. But you don't want to drive that far."

"I might have to," Faye muttered and went to wipe Gabby's face. "Sorry about that, Agatha. She's a spitter. I'll take her back whenever you want."

"I can go another hour or two," Agatha said cheerfully, but she rose and handed Faye her baby. "Here you go. She wants you."

A phone pinged, and Jenny looked down. "That's me." She checked the screen. "It's the history department at the university. Hang on." She rose and walked a few steps down the beach to answer.

"Why is she working on the weekend?" Agatha asked critically. "Especially when she's with friends?"

Faye's eyes were following her friend. "She's been waiting for a call," she confided. "In fact, we came out here to make the waiting easier." That and the tension in her voice let Barbara know that it wasn't just any old call. It was an important call.

She leaned forward. She didn't gossip often, but sometimes, she let herself be pulled into the river of local news and scandal. "Why has she been waiting for a call from her department? Is it about a student?"

Faye shook her head. "Not about a student. It's about herself."

"Herself," Barbara repeated. "A pay raise? She's only an adjunct at the university, isn't she?"

Too focused on her friend to answer, Faye rose with the baby in her arms because Jenny was coming back. "And?" Faye asked breathlessly.

Jenny stooped, and a deep breath lifted her chest. "Yes." She broke into laughter. "Yes! Faye, I got it!"

"Got what?" Christy asked, her voice rising with alarm. "What did you get, Jenny?"

Jenny let the breath she'd been holding go with an almighty whoosh. Her shoulders relaxed, and she smiled. "I've got a tenure-track position. I applied for it last fall, and the dean just offered it to me."

Everyone broke into applause. Barbara rose with everyone else to wish Jenny congratulations and good luck. "You deserve it, my dear," Barbara whispered into the younger woman's ear when she embraced her. "Good luck."

"This means they can't fire you anymore, doesn't it?" Agatha asked when it was her turn.

"Well, once I have tenure. Then they can't fire me for doing the kind of research I think is important," Jenny amended. "Tenure only protects my research. They can still fire me if I slack off or am mean to the students."

"I heard the students like you." Christy pressed a kiss on Jenny's cheek. "Congratulations."

"Thank you." Eyes beaming, Jenny went to pick up her purse. "Faye, can we go back? I want to tell Jon and the kids, and I have to send my official response and talk to the head of the department."

"Yes. Please. I'd love to get home so Gabby can nap in the crib, not the car." Faye rose and started to strap the baby into the car seat that was waiting under the table.

Jenny grabbed the diaper bag from a chair. "Listen, everyone—I'm sorry to break us up for now. Jon said he'd throw me a party if I got the job, so I bet there'll soon be a get-together at the winery."

"What if Jon has changed his mind?" Agatha asked.

"I really don't think he will. But on the off chance he does..." Jenny brushed her hair behind her ear and grinned happily. "...I'll throw myself a party. Make sure to come!"

A moment later, the two women stormed off toward the small parking lot, laughing and chatting, flushed rosy and very busy indeed.

Barbara turned back to her friends. She'd been about to say how glad she was to see Jenny so happy, but the look on their faces made her exhale without saying it. "What's going on?"

"Oh. Hmm." Christy pushed her sunglasses higher on her nose. "I was just thinking how nice it'll be for Jenny to fully be part of the history department now. She's starting a whole new career she loves. Not every woman gets to do that."

"I was thinking the same," Agatha murmured. "It's nice to know you're needed, isn't it?"

Thoughtfully, Barbara nodded. Christy had only just left a career she truly loved. And Agatha needed to see her family more often.

Her car arrived back in the lot, and Lukas got out, holding a large, yellow manila folder.

He came striding toward her, and Barbara felt a certain sense of relief that he was back. However old the man was, he showed no signs of his age other than the deep laugh lines by his eyes and the silver at his temples. In fact, he seemed fitter than many of the younger men she'd employed.

"I brought the blueprints." Lukas held out the humble folder.

"Thank you very much." Barbara took the folder and opened it to check that it was indeed the prints for the cottage. "Good, that's exactly what we needed." She pushed them back and handed the pack to Christy. "Here you go. Now you can get Ethan to look at them and renovate your cottage to your heart's content."

CHAPTER 12

I'm going to go to his house." Christy tugged her white silk blouse into the new jeans. She couldn't remember the last time she owned denim. "Do you like how they look?" Critically, she turned in front of the mirror. She'd need some time to get used to her new look.

"Yes, I do. The jeans look nice and normal, unlike your business clothes." Agatha was leaning against the door jamb of Christy's room, her arms crossed. "Why are you meeting him at his house?"

"We are not meeting. I'm stopping by."

"Why?"

Christy glanced at her friend. "Because I want his opinion on the bathroom wall. And for that, I have to drop off the blueprints. Since he's doing me a favor, I can't very well ask him to come down here to get them himself."

"Didn't you offer to pay him?"

"Of course I did. But he refused to take my money." Christy decided against lipstick. Her signature red lips didn't seem so important now that she no longer needed to brand herself. Instead, she used the honey vanilla lip balm she'd picked up at the clothing store's register and swiped a barely visible streak of pearl eyeshadow onto her lids. She tucked a silver curl behind her ear. "I think I like how this looks too. Interesting."

"Hmm." Agatha was chewing on her lip. "If he won't take money, you should at least take him out for dinner. Architects don't come cheap."

"I'll play it by ear." Ethan had had a second, more thorough look at the house, but Christy hadn't seen him since. She rubbed her lips to distribute the chapstick, tasting a burst of honey vanilla. Ready, she turned to leave the room.

"Hey. Don't forget that." Agatha nodded at the manila folder on Christy's dresser.

"Right." Christy turned back to grab it. "It's the reason I'm going, isn't it?"

"Mh-hmm. That's what you said." Agatha shook her head. "I think you still like him."

"I've always liked him." Christy wished she'd kept their history to herself. But there was no way to keep anything from Agatha. They had both had too much red wine last night, and Christy wasn't used to drinking. "Like I said, that wasn't the problem. But that's all over. Don't mention it, please. It's a sore spot."

"Okay." Agatha stepped aside so Christy could pass. "How are the renovations coming along?"

"Good. I have electricity now." Christy went down the stairs, feeling a little like a teenager trying to sneak out. "Which is great. River showed me how to use some tools, and we just worked out how to refinish the wood floors. It's fun, actually. And a good workout. Also good stretching because once you seal the floor, you can't step on it again until it's dry. It's like a big game of Twister."

"Did you play by yourself, or did Ethan play Twister too?"

"Agatha, you're the worst. Of course I was doing it by myself. The floors should be dry today. After I drop off the blueprints, I'll go back and see what I can do with the bathroom. I do need it to be bigger than it is right now, so I thought I'd take out the second linen cabinet."

"You'll take down a solid wall?"

"I don't think it's solid. I bet it's just a frame and drywall. It was probably added fairly recently, but I just want Ethan to look at the blueprint and make sure I can take it down without the ceiling collapsing." Christy stepped into her new, practical sneakers and opened the front door.

"Good luck."

Christy turned around. "What are you going to do, Agatha?"

"I'm going to open all the windows in the kitchen, bake, and listen to my audiobook." Agatha smiled. "I can't wait. Get out."

Christy laughed. "I'm gone. You have fun. I'll see you tonight." Soon, she could move out and get out of Agatha's hair. Living together worked out better than expected, but they were both used to their own space and lots of privacy.

Agatha waved and closed the door, and Christy turned and walked through the front yard. It was still morning, but a golden sun had already warmed the air and awoken a kaleidoscope of colors around the old cottage.

Christy's favorites were the vibrant roses in red, pink, and white, as well as the lavender bushes with their soothing fragrance that nestled in between old rhododendrons. There were also bright orange poppies and delicate azaleas, their green leaves hidden under clouds of blossoms. Sweet daisies—Agatha's favorites—dotted the ground where the old wooden fence separated the property from the street, and clematis vines wound around the posts in bright shades of purples and blues.

She climbed in her car and punched Ethan's address into her GPS. The drive led her through town, across to the island, and up a hill. His street ran to the tip of a bluff, and it was dotted with a handful of large, rather modern houses. Based on looks, he'd done very well for himself. Even in Mendocino, houses like these were expensive.

His house was a sleek affair built on top of a smooth outcropping, while his double-wide garage sat below the house, on level with the street.

Christy pulled up to the curb in front of it, gathered her phone and the manila envelope, and got out.

The sea breeze was more noticeable out here. She brushed her hair back and climbed the wide bluestone stairs that led to the house. In contrast to Agatha's colorful, rambling garden, Ethan had opted for simplicity, planting eucalyptus trees, yucca, and agave to create a peaceful, coastal atmosphere around his house.

When she reached the door, she paused to catch her breath. The stairs were not so steep. But it was strange, seeing Ethan's house. It suddenly occurred to Christy that he might have a wife, a lady friend, or kids. Or someone...

When her panting had calmed into deeper, more regular breaths, she knocked.

It didn't take long before the door opened. "Yes?"

"Hi, Ethan. It's me. Christy."

"Christy." The door opened wider, and Ethan appeared. He was wearing a white button-down shirt, sleeves rolled to the elbows, and light linen pants. His feet were bare and as tan as his hands and arms. "Hey. What brings you over here?"

"I wanted to drop off the blueprints for the cottage." She held out the envelope. "If you're still willing to look at them, that is."

"Sure." He took the envelope and raked a hand through his hair. "Erm..."

She held up her hand. "Say no more. I'm on my way." She turned but stopped when he touched her arm. "Yes?" His touch tingled. She shifted away, and he let go.

"Christy..." His blue eyes held her gaze.

"Yes, Ethan?"

"I was... Is someone waiting for you?" He glanced at the street below them.

"Nobody is waiting for me. I came in my own car," she said. Too late did she notice that she was cupping the spot where he'd touched her. Quickly, she dropped her hand.

"Do you have time for a cup of tea?"

"Yes, I suppose." Truth be told, Christy wanted to see his house. She wanted to know how he lived. "Um. Do you have family inside?"

He smiled, but the smile didn't reach his eyes. "I'm not married," he said. "No kids. Not even a dog, to be honest. Until a couple of years ago, I was traveling too much. Now I could get one, but...I don't know. I can't decide if I want pets or not."

"Hmm." Christy had also never been able to decide whether she wanted a cat enough to get one. Several times she'd been on the brink of adopting one, only to chicken out again. She smiled. "I know what you mean."

He stepped aside to let her in. "I was about to have tea anyway. The water is already hot."

Christy stepped into the house. She was greeted by an abundance of windows framing panoramic views of the coast. Everywhere she looked, the warmth of natural woods seamlessly integrated with the sleekness of carefully chosen metals. "Oh, what a beautiful place." She turned, eager to see it all. "You designed this?"

He closed the door. "I did."

"Well, it's marvelous. A perfectly balanced blend of modern aesthetics and natural elements. I love it."

"Would you like a tour?" Christy did want a tour, and Ethan led the way, striding barefooted across the polished hardwood floors. After a short hesitation, Christy also kicked off her shoes and followed.

Maybe it was the contrast to her own little cottage, with which she'd become so familiar in the last few days. But the place took her breath away. It was large, airy, and quietly luxurious.

Most walls had large windows that let natural light flood the rooms. The living room had a modern minimalist fireplace, modern comfortable furniture, and sliding glass doors onto a spacious deck overlooking the Pacific Ocean. Christy could have stayed out here all day, gazing at the play of the waves. But Ethan, clearly used to the stunning view, walked on.

"Erm, this is the kitchen." Ethan gestured at an open kitchen perfect for entertaining. The adjacent dining area had a floor-to-ceiling window that showed sunlight filtering through tall, airy eucalyptus trees. "And upstairs." He climbed a floating staircase to the upper level, where Christy caught glimpses of several bedrooms and a calming, serene bathroom that belonged on the pages of a spa magazine.

But what attracted Christy's attention almost more than any of the beautiful architecture or tasteful interior design were the paintings hanging on the wall. "Goodness." Christy stepped closer to admire an abstract landscape in the staircase. "Is that who I think it is?"

Ethan joined her on the landing. "I bought it in—"

"New York, Cardan Gallery auction, 1989," Christy finished for him. She also knew the eye-watering amount of money the abstract had sold for.

"Yes, that's right." Ethan smiled. "You're good."

She glanced at him. "I'm not so sure. I missed a whopper last December."

"I read about that."

She shrugged. "Well, it's true. I wasn't doing well at the time because an old friend had just passed away. But that's no excuse."

He raised an eyebrow. "A bridge I built once collapsed. And I wasn't distracted or grieving when I built it. I *just* messed up."

Her eyes widened. "Oh no!"

He nodded. "Sheer luck nobody was hurt. I still wake up every morning grateful for that grace. But the financial loss was staggering. I was ready to resign, leave the country, whatever it took to relieve the crushing shame I felt. But I'd learned a lesson from...before." He glanced at her.

She tilted her head. Was he talking about her? "What was the lesson?"

"Running doesn't help." His voice was low. "So I stayed and worked through it with the community. It was the best decision I ever made, and, in a way, it launched my career."

She turned to another painting on the wall. It, too, was an exquisite piece of art, but her eyes could do hardly more than trace the flow of the lines. Finally she gave up and turned to face him. "I believe I detect another meaning in your words. Are you saying I was running away after you kissed Abby?"

He ran a hand through his hair. "I'm talking about myself."

Christy held a tense breath. "I'm no longer a naive undergrad student with a broken heart. Tell me about it, Ethan."

"Tell you about what, Christy?"

"The past." She crossed her arms. He made a motion as if to reach out to her but didn't. She let go of the uncomfortable breath. "We are neighbors now, Ethan. I'd like to finally know what really happened between you and my sister."

CHAPTER 13

F or a few moments, Ethan studied her face, his blue eyes sky bright and serious. "Let's go outside," he said. "I'll make us that cup of tea, and we'll sit in the sun and talk."

Christy nodded, secretly relieved he wasn't going to run from the conversation any more than from the collapsed bridge.

They walked back outside, and Ethan took a moment to brew a pot of tea. He also brought a plate of cookies outside and set it on the glass table on the deck. "Is the umbrella good?" He tilted the large market umbrella hanging over them.

"Yes, thank you. I'm perfectly comfortable." But somehow, even though the past was the past and that was that—her heart was still pattering like dog claws on a wood floor.

"So." Ethan poured them both a cup of steaming, fragrant tea and sat. "What would you like to know about the past, Christy?" His face was carefully smooth, but his eyes were kind enough to encourage her.

She lifted her teacup and sipped. It was a smoky tea, full of fragrance and spice.

He pushed the plate over. "These are maple pecan cookies, my favorite with this tea. Try one."

She sat down her cup and looked at him. "I would like to know what happened with you and Abby all those years back."

"It was what I told you, Christy. I promise."

She shook her head. "I don't need your promise, Ethan. Just the truth."

"That's the truth. There was never more than the one drunken kiss you saw. That was it."

She sighed. "I was so in love with you, stupid little me."

He shook his head. "You aren't stupid. Not now, not then. I was. I was stupid, and drunk, and I was waiting for you when Abby arrived. She wanted to pick up a book or something, and she'd been drinking too. And I..." He shook his head. "Like I said, I was the one being stupid."

"You don't have to lie." Abby and she had been sisters, but so different.

"I have no reason to lie, Christy," he said softly. "What would I gain from it now? The damage was done a long time ago." The lines in his face showed that he was being truthful.

Slowly, Christy nodded. But she wasn't done yet. Maybe there'd been only one kiss. But it wasn't all out in the open air yet. He was still holding something back, she sensed. "You've been in contact with her, haven't you? I doubt one drunken kiss is enough of a reason to stay in touch for years."

He leaned back, his eyes hiding nothing. "Yes, we stayed in touch. We became...friends. Sort of."

"Ah." Christy was surprised that the admission still had the power to sting her heart.

"I liked Abby. I'm not going to apologize for that. But nothing romantic ever happened between us." He looked up, his eyes testing her. "I don't count that kiss because it wasn't romantic. Not one bit."

"Well." Christy played with her cup, turning it in her fingers. "Seeing her kiss my boyfriend was what broke the camel's back for us back then. We were just too different. In the years that followed, I tried to get back in touch. But she wasn't interested. She never reciprocated."

There was a short pause. Then, "Abby had problems," Ethan said gently. "I don't know how much you know about that, but from my conversations with her...my guess is that she kept it all from you."

"She probably did. She never told me anything about herself. Only the superficial things, you know, but she never talked about her feelings or her struggles." Some sisters fought as kids and later grew into friendship and sisterhood, but not the two of them. Abby had never confided in Christy, always treating her like the annoying little sister instead. "Well, she had you to talk to."

She held up her hand before he could protest. "I don't mean to sound bitter. I loved Abby in my own way; she was family and still the only sister I ever had. I sincerely wish we wouldn't have had that fight back then. But I loved you." She shook her head. However many birthdays she added to her collection, she'd never get used to how powerful a force first love was. She cleared her throat and looked up, almost embarrassed to still be harping the point. But she wanted him to understand how differently she would have acted back then had she not been dazed and confused. "I was such a baby."

"As far as I remember, you were perfectly grown up." He smiled, and then he leaned forward. "You never told me that you loved me, Christy. Not once."

Christy shrugged. "You'd better believe I congratulated myself for not doing it after I saw you with my sister."

Ethan fell back in his chair again and sighed. "In no way am I defending myself. I felt terrible. I knew I'd done wrong, Christy." He took a deep breath. "Okay. Erm, let's do this."

"Do what?" She had known he was holding back—here it was, the thing that really mattered. Christy squared her shoulders. "Tell me, please."

"Okay." He crossed his arms in a gesture of defeat. "Did you know that your sister struggled with alcohol?"

"She liked to drink, obviously. She certainly struggled that night I saw you two. But she wasn't an alcoholic."

"No," he said gently. "She *was* an alcoholic. High functioning, but...she knew she had a problem. And she did what she could to take care of it. But she didn't always win the battle."

"What?" Christy's throat was dry. "I never heard her as much as mention it."

"Don't forget that, just like Abby, I was drunk too. Then you left me, and I..." He shook his head. "I loved you too, you know."

Now it was Christy who folded her arms. "What are you saying?"

"I made every single heartbreaking mistake a young man can make, Christy. My head was full of dumb images and ideas about who I wanted to be."

That softened her again. She, too, had had those ideas of herself, only to have them crushed by life and circumstances. Rebuilding according to reality was never easy. "Who did you want to be?"

He shook his head. "A hotshot, skipping footloose and fancy-free through Haight-Ashbury with all the other hippies, while also somehow getting the girl I loved and maintaining top grades." He shrugged. "Well, let me tell you, life checked me on my expectations. I was a hot mess, not a hotshot. And I'm still sorry for the damage I did."

"Yeah." A smile tugged on her lips because clearly, he had recovered just fine. But the news about Abby still burned in her throat. She had so many questions...

"After you left, I fell into a very vulnerable place. I was down and out for the count, and I certainly wasn't interested in romancing Abby or any other girl, for that matter. But it's one of those twists." He shifted his weight as he remembered. "Exactly *because* I was down and out and vulnerable, Abby felt she could confide in me. She was just realizing that her drinking was more than a fun, social activity to blow off steam. She'd already tried to stop and failed once, and she was ashamed of breaking her promise to herself. She needed someone to confide in, and she instinctively felt that I was in no position to judge."

Christy felt her eyes widen. "You really are serious about Abby being an alcoholic. I can't believe it."

"She asked me to go to support meetings with her because she didn't feel safe going alone," Ethan said and looked up. "And in another one of those twists, I often thought she saved me. I wasn't on the brink the way she was, but if she hadn't asked me to listen to those stories...who knows. I was on a slippery slope."

"You went to AA meetings with Abby?" Christy's brain had to take new turns, and she felt like she was lagging behind.

Ethan nodded. "Until I graduated and got a job. And even afterward, we stayed in touch, calling a couple times a year to catch up. She told me you knew about that."

Christy held up a hand. "The car accident. Was she drunk? I never heard that she was, but apparently, I know nothing of what's really going on. Maybe her husband decided not to share it?"

Ethan shook his head. "She was not."

"Did she... How was she before the accident?" Christy still had trouble accepting it. She hadn't known her own sister well enough to see that she needed help.

That was a much bigger failure than misjudging a piece of art.

"As far as I know, she was doing okay. We weren't in touch then, which was always a good sign. Our relationship revolved mostly around her battle with addiction." He looked at his hands. "The struggle never goes away. But it got easier. She had a husband she loved, and she adored her daughters. I believed her when she said her family kept her on the straight and narrow."

"You were there for her when I wasn't." Christy set her elbows on the table and buried her face in her hands. "I wish someone had told me. I wish I'd known she was struggling."

"She forbade me to tell you. She didn't have to since I was probably the last person you'd have asked. Of course she knew you didn't answer my calls, but she really wanted to keep this from you."

Christy dropped her hands. Her denial was suddenly pierced by anger. How had Abby dared to keep her out? It was another betrayal again! "Well, she was wrong. You told me after all."

Unaware of the anger boiling under the words, Ethan smiled. "It's been a minute, hasn't it? And, as you say, now that we're neighbors...it's important to me that you know how it really was. Abby and I didn't have a torrid affair. I drove her to AA meetings. We talked a couple times a year. That's what happened." His face turned serious as he held her gaze. "And apparently, you and I loved each other."

Christy reached out and fished a maple pecan cookie from the plate. She nibbled on it. Not because she was hungry, but because she wanted a sensory experience other than what she was feeling.

"More tea?" he asked after a while.

"Please. I'm thirsty." She held out her cup. Already, she was simmering down. It wasn't his fault; he'd tried to do right by Abby. Unlike Christy herself. No—that wasn't entirely correct. Her insides softened as denial and anger morphed into something more mature. She *had* tried. She'd called, she'd written, she'd send her nieces gifts. It had been Abby who had intentionally kept her out.

"You and Abby never made up, did you?" His voice interrupted her thoughts. "I'm afraid the real crime I committed was driving you two apart."

She glanced at him and drank, letting the smoky flavor fill her mouth. "Crime?"

He nodded. "I think I pitched sister against sister at the worst possible moment. And you two never made up."

Christy set down her cup. This discussion was much more complex than she'd anticipated. "That's what I thought too," she finally admitted. "But now I don't know anymore. Abby must have had another reason not to stay in touch." She looked at her hands, old now, with skinny veins rising like rivers on a map. "She didn't want me to know about her addiction. She didn't want to show me that side of her. She preferred to live life without her sister."

"Maybe." Slowly, Ethan reached out and covered her hand with his own. Its size and warmth felt eerily familiar. "Or maybe, she wanted to let *you* live your life without her," he said, his voice as soft as a warm night. "She wanted to spare you the darkness that often overwhelmed her. She was a good person, Christy. She did the best she could."

Suddenly, Christy's face crumpled, and her lip trembled. Whether it was the touch of Ethan's hand, or the shocking news about Abby, or the thought that her sister had loved her after all, Christy didn't know.

Without commenting, Ethan pulled out the napkin under the cookie plate, shook it out, and handed it to Christy. "I know," he said. "I cried for Abby too. Many times."

Christy nodded, crunching the napkin in her hand. "Thank you," she whispered. "I didn't know it, but my sister needed you so much more than I. It changes everything."

Despite the frown line appearing between his eyes, Ethan smiled. "So, how are your nieces?"

Christy's shoulders sagged as she turned to the sea. "I have no idea. We lost contact. I have no address or phone number, and if they're on any social media platforms, I haven't found them yet."

Surprised, he lifted an eyebrow. "You can't reach them?" She shook her head, and he pulled out his phone. "What's your number?" he asked, sliding his open contacts over to her. "I'll send you their contacts."

Christy stared at his phone. Could it be that easy? She sucked in a breath and almost laughed with nerves. "And here I just wanted to drop off the cottage blueprints."

He smiled. "Too much?"

Grateful that he understood, she smiled back. "To be honest, it's a lot to take in." She picked up the phone and tapped her information into the form before handing it back to him. "I wish…"

"Yes?" The blue look he gave her came straight from a different lifetime. "What's that?"

"I wish we had met years ago." Christy stood, ready to leave. "Ethan, I'm going to go. I have a lot to think about. I need some time alone."

He rose too. "Wait. Wait." He took a step toward her. "Where are you going?"

"I don't know. My cottage."

He hesitated. "Alone, at the cottage? Are you sure?"

She looked at him, surprised. What were the alternatives? She was in her sixties. She had long ago given up on finding someone to hold her when she was overwhelmed or stressed; everyone had to sort out their own affairs.

"Stay," he said. "I'll make you dinner, and we'll look at the blueprints."

She looked at him for a while, taking in his eyes, the laugh lines, the smile on his lips. "No," she said softly. "But thank you. I'd really rather be alone." She turned and went inside, finding her way through the house to the front door, down the blue stone steps, into her car.

Strapping herself in, she ducked her head to glance up at the deck. She hadn't expected to see him, but there he stood, leaning on the railing and looking straight into her eyes.

Christy blinked and started her car. Ethan waved once before she drove off, but she felt his kind blue eyes follow her all the way down the bluff.

CHAPTER 14

"He said it was okay to take it down? Are you sure?" Agatha experimentally knocked on the wall in the bathroom. It sounded hollow. "If it was me, I'd keep the second linen cabinet. You can't have enough of them."

"But I want the space. I like a big bathroom; I want at least one claw-footed bathtub somewhere in this house. Ethan checked the blueprint and texted to say it was fine." Christy picked up the small sledgehammer they'd found in the lean-to. "Here, step out of the way. I don't want a flying piece of drywall to hit you. I know it's hollow because there's a little panel inside the linen cabinet that opens for access. The wall might splinter."

Agatha stepped out of the way, and Christy swung the heavy hammer. With a soul-shaking recoil, it cracked the wall. Paint flakes toppled to the ground like monochrome confetti, and stale dust swirled in the air.

"Dear me." Agatha's grin was visible even though she was covering her mouth with the sleeve of her purple sweatshirt. "I had no idea you had so much rage in you."

Christy grinned and lifted the hammer for an encore. "Watch me."

"I am. Oh!" Agatha flinched as Christy landed another blow. "Hang on. Hang on. Stop." She held up her hand.

Christy lowered her weapon. "What?"

"There's something inside the wall."

"What, like insulation?"

Agatha scoffed. "Dream on. You won't find a shred of glass fiber in these cottage walls. No, it's something else. I'm going to pull it out."

"Go on. Do it." Christy leaned on her war hammer. To be honest, she probably couldn't lift the heavy thing many more times. She didn't mind a break. "Maybe someone put it into the wall from the linen cabinet and shoved it too high to retrieve it. Or they simply forgot about it."

"Don't whack me." Agatha shoved the cracked bits of wall out of the way.

"Sheesh, Agatha. Trust. It's so important."

"I know I am, but what are you?" Agatha peeked into the dark hole and gingerly reached into the crack. "Please tell me it's not hair? It's...no, it's string."

"Goodness." Christy shivered. "Thank heaven it's string."

Agatha chuckled. "Here, I got it." Carefully, she pulled, trying to see into the dark. "It's bigger than I thought."

"Sometimes people find treasure in their walls," Christy said. "There was a case in Sweden where somebody found an old oil painting worth a million dollars inside a bricked-up closet."

"A cool million? Maybe I should check my own walls." Agatha wiggled her find free and set it on the clean, dry floor by the bathtub. "It's a bunch of paper. Oh! They're letters, Christy. Somebody put a bunch of letters in there when they built the linen closet."

"Really?" Christy knelt beside Agatha. Her joints cracked. "Augh." She rubbed the spot.

"Knees not what they used to be, huh?" Agatha glanced at her friend. "I'm keeping fit with gardening and housework, but you still need to find an exercise routine you enjoy."

"I'm renovating an entire house, Agatha." Christy picked up the top letters. "The name on the envelope is written in black ink," she observed. "It's faded now. And there's no address, as if the writer didn't know where to send the letter."

"What's the name? I can't read it without my glasses."

"Hmm." Christy held the letter at arm's length. "James. I think."

"James... All right. Open it. What's it say?"

Christy flipped the unsealed envelope open and pulled out the folded letter. "Let's see." She rose with a groan and sat on the rim of the bathtub. Her eyes flew over the page.

"What. Does. It. Say?" Agatha asked impatiently. "Come on, Christy!"

"It's a love letter." Smiling, Christy flipped the page over. "It's a love letter to a person named James."

"Really?" Agatha asked eagerly. "Great. Read it to me."

"Fine." Christy took a breath and read.

My dearest James,

I miss you. I miss your laughter and your arms, the silly jokes that only you find amusing, and the way your eyes crinkle when you smile. My memories are my lifeline, shrinking the miles that keep us apart. If I could just have you back, I would no longer care if they found us out. It's too late for me, anyway. I love you that much.

Well, since you ask...I love you even more.

Do you remember when we danced on the beach? When you return, we will waltz in the moonshine again. Or maybe you'll teach me a new dance you learned abroad. I promise not to step on your toes again. I guess I forgot to look at my feet last time. But I'm not to blame. Your lips claimed all my attention that night.

I lie sleepless at night, wondering where you are. Can you see the stars where you are, or is there dust and debris in the air? Do you have a bed or only the floor of a British bomb shelter? Are you safe? Please be safe. I wish my love could wrap around you like the briar hedge that guarded Sleeping Beauty for a hundred long years. Do you think briar roses can secure the front, if there would be enough of them? Anyway. I'm tired and half-asleep all the time since you left, and no matter how much I sleep, I don't feel refreshed. I'm going to bed now, darling, to dream of you. I think only your kiss can truly wake me up, so be a duck and hurry back to me.

All my kisses,
Doris

"Ah. Young love in the time of war." Agatha sighed happily, flipping through the other envelopes. "So Doris wrote these letters to her boyfriend. What a romantic find, Christy!"

"Who is Doris?" Christy looked up. "Sounds familiar."

"I have no idea. Wait. Doris...Doris." The light of recognition dawned in Agatha's eyes at the same moment Christy remembered where she'd heard the name before. Agatha stood, her eyes wide. "I'm going to give Barbara a call."

"Yes." Christy also rose, giving her knees time to unfurl from their cramped position. She actually felt less stiff now than when she'd first arrived, but still the decades had taken a toll. She gently folded the old letter and slipped it back into the envelope. "Come on. Let's call Barbara together."

While Agatha talked to their friend on speaker, Christy listened and carried the love letters into the kitchen. She carefully brushed the dust and plaster off the sepia paper and into the bin, then set the letters on the table where they couldn't get wet.

Luckily, the truck with her things had arrived, and many of her friends in Mendocino Cove had come over to help her unload and unpack them. Boxes and random furniture were still strewn throughout the house, but the kitchen was almost done.

Christy took a moment to look around. The sunlight glowed on the soft, wide boards of the newly refinished pine floor and danced on the pearl-white walls that she had finished painting just the night before. Lush spider plants and trailing pothos brightened corners and edges, and two white-and-purple orchids added a grateful touch. Christy's collection of simple charcoal drawings on the walls and a few antique silver figurines sitting on shelves and windowsills completed the look.

The longer she looked at her cozy haven, the more the contrast of art and rustic setting delighted her. The fridge and stove were hooked up and working, and she had bought an adorable wooden kitchen table and matching chairs at Faye's second-hand store. The set was a perfect fit for the space and the first real kitchen table she'd ever owned.

She put on the kettle, and while she waited for the tea water to boil, Christy went out the new door Jon and his cousins had just put in. It led into the overgrown garden where she picked a bouquet of lavender and delicate white blossoms with a honey-like scent. Then she rummaged through boxes until she found a vase. The green art deco-pattern complemented the sweet-smelling bouquet perfectly. Christy filled it and set it on the table.

After that was done, she unwrapped her tea set from the newspapers that had protected it and washed the cups and plates in the deep porcelain sink while thinking about poor Doris, wondering why the letters had ended up in the hidey-hole in the wall. By the time she dried her cups with the pretty new kitchen towel Jenny had gifted her, Christy surprised herself by humming a little melody.

In her old city apartment, Christy had rarely spent time in her kitchen and even less time thinking about it. But now, she loved the old-world charm of her cottage kitchen.

Once the table was set, Christy opened the window that looked out on the garden, the beach, and the sapphire sea. The salty, warm, tangy sea breeze blew in, curious and ready to play with the short, gauzy curtains that had been Hazel's housewarming gift.

Smiling, she poured boiling water onto the fragrant loose tea she'd found at the local market. No more coffee for her. That was the old life; that was over. From now on, she'd sleep in every morning, long enough that she didn't need coffee black as death to wake her up. Instead, she'd take her time making tea and sipping it while looking out at the every-changing sea.

"Happy?" Agatha was coming into the kitchen, carrying a tall torte in her hands. "The room did turn out beautifully. Kitchens are so important, aren't they?"

"I was wondering where you'd got to." Christy smiled. "Did you really go over to your house to get a cake?"

"I thought I might as well." Agatha set her gift on the table. "Barbara needs a few minutes to get here. I'm hungry. I want cake. And since you can't bake, it had to be me."

Christy laughed. "What did you bring?"

"A strawberry-almond torte. I had to use up all that cream and the glazed splintered almonds I had left."

"I hope the berries are from your garden." A lot of berries had ripened in the last week, and a flood of delicious desserts had danced through Agatha's kitchen.

"Always. I'm drowning in them, not that that's a complaint." Agatha cut the cake into sumptuous slices. "It's pretty simple. Just layers of sponge, cream whipped with vanilla sugar, slightly frozen strawberry bits, roasted almond, and, um, a *touch* of rum, actually."

"Sounds more delicious than simple." The scent of fresh strawberries mingled with the honey-scent of the white flowers and the wild fragrance the light breeze carried in from the sparkling Pacific. Christy inhaled deeply, and her stomach grumbled. "Hmm. When does Barbara get here?"

Just then, car tires crunched the gravel at the side of the road. "Aha," Christy said. "Perfect timing. Everything is ready."

A few moments later, Barbara walked into the kitchen, nodding at her friends. "My aunt's letters." Her smile was strained. "May I please read them?"

CHAPTER 15

"Here they are." Christy lifted the bundle of letters from the table and held them out.

"Oh my goodness." With a grateful glance, Barbara took them. Her heart was beating in a hard staccato rhythm, and it wasn't only because she'd practically raced down to Mendocino Cove. Why was there a hidden cache of letters from a beloved aunt who had died too young in a freak accident? Was there one addressed to Barbara? Were there family secrets that would unsettle the order of things?

She smiled an apology. "Sorry for being in a state," she said. "I can't believe you found this. I have no idea what this is about." The stack was maybe ten or twelve letters tall, and the paper felt old and dry in her hands. "Thanks for calling right away."

"You're welcome." Smiling, Christy reached out to pull her in for a quick squeeze, then went back to the sink to pull the tea leaf egg out of a gorgeous antique Korean tea pot.

Her friend's smile had changed since she got here, Barbara suddenly noticed. It used to be kind but thin-lipped, as much business as joy. Just like the impeccably tailored pinstripe suits and black heels. Now, her smile had become wider, showing in her eyes and making her face look younger and more vulnerable.

Barbara inhaled. The air smelled clean and fragrant, of strawberries and cream, flowers and beach. She let the breath go again, relaxing her shoulders and her diaphragm. "Okay. Calm, calm." She chuckled at herself and held up the letters. "I just couldn't believe... I do apologize for rushing in here like this."

Christy looked over her shoulder, still smiling. "Barb, it's no problem. You can rush in any time you like."

"But it's your new house! I was so muddled to hear Doris's name crop up like that. I'm being terribly rude." Barbara set the letters back down on the table. There was time to read them later. They had been hidden from the world for decades. A few more moments would not matter. She made herself look around, getting a general impression of light and cleanliness and comfort. "Goodness, you've done wonders. It's beautiful. Congratulations, my dear."

"Thank you, I'm quite happy with how it turned out." Christy laughed. "But you are used to magnificent halls, endless corridors, and sweeping staircases. You don't have to be polite."

Agatha pulled out one of the chairs. "Sheesh, Christy." She shook her head. "Barbara isn't being polite when she says she likes what you've done. She's got too much money to pretend things." She turned to her friend. "Isn't that right, Barbara?"

"Well, I don't know if it's entirely true," Barbara said, feeling more cheerful already. Nothing like one of Agatha's straight shots to lift the spirit! "But I'd say there's a kernel of truth to it." The tension in her shoulders eased; the longer she was in the kitchen, the better she felt. With a sigh of relief, she sat as well in one of the comfortable chairs, only now noticing the fresh paint and gleaming floor, the sunlight and floral aroma, the silver and flowers and art that brightened the room and nourished the mind. "This cottage may not have endless corridors and sweeping staircases—"

"What it *does* have is a hole in the bathroom wall and lots of unpacked boxes." Christy chuckled.

"But it is a cottage for the heart," Barbara finished. "A peaceful place by the sea where you can bake and garden and drink tea with friends."

"You can also read here or do arts and crafts on the table," Agatha added. "You could even unpack the boxes, if you had to. Just saying."

"She just moved in, Agatha. Give the woman a break." Barbara threw her a stern look to not be impatient. Their common friend was doing very well.

Christy chuckled as she washed her hands. "I think what Agatha here is *really* saying is that she's hungry. Let's have some of the cream torte she so kindly brought."

"You made this? My word. Margrit couldn't do it better." And just like that, Agatha was forgiven for making fun of Barbara's compliment.

"You want some?" Agatha, as always perfectly un-bothered by stern glances, lifted a layered slice off the plate.

Barbara smiled. "Yes, fine. I'll have one of your slices. Go on." She held out her plate, and then Christy's, and Agatha's own, and Agatha plopped a juicy portion on each.

"So." Christy brought over the teapot and poured. "Now, Barbara."

"Yes." Barbara sipped the tea, finding it to be both refreshing and tasty. "What?"

Christy glanced at her. "Why would your aunt's letters be inside my bathroom wall?"

Agatha raised her fork. "Barbara's aunt used to live in this cottage, Barb. Where else would she hide her letters, huh?"

"She did live here," Barbara confirmed. "Of course it's ages ago now." She tasted her cake. It danced across her taste buds like summer itself, sun-drenched and light-footed. "This is very good," she said to Agatha. "Very good indeed."

"Thank you. It's a break from lemon tarts," Agatha agreed.

Christy resumed her own journey through cream and berries and tender sponge cake. "Well, I knew that already," she mumbled, her mouth full. "We did talk about your aunt... But why the bathroom wall?"

"Well, we can't ask her, can we?" Barbara had had enough cream to clot her brain. She gave up on finishing the large slice.

"I don't like unsolved mysteries. They keep me up at night. What else is in my walls?"

"Nothing." Agatha also put down her fork and leaned back, eyeing the leftover with regret in her eyes. "That was the only wall with a hidey-hole. She opened it from the laundry closet."

"Maybe there's a clue in the letters," Barbara said and glanced at her aunt's secret.

Christy took a sip of her fragrant tea. "Are you going to read the letters now?"

"If you don't mind. I can't wait any longer." Barbara straightened her back and wiggled the first few letters free. "It's probably nothing, right?"

"Who knows. That's the one we read already." Agatha pointed at the letter on top. "Before we realized that it was Doris who wrote them. We didn't open the rest."

Barbara put the open letter aside. She'd read it later since Agatha had already told her on the phone what it was about. She picked up the second letter and turned it over. Unlike the first, this envelope was sealed. There was no address on it, only the name—James.

"Hang on." Christy got up and went to a hand-thrown cup that held pens and pencils. "Here." She pulled out a letter opener and brought it back to the table. Taking her seat, she handed it to Barbara. "Try this."

"This is ivory." The slim letter opener with the sharp edge felt warm and smooth in Barbara's hand. "Beautiful."

"I promise it's very old. Four hundred years at least. It's from a palace in China."

"You have so much weird stuff," Agatha noted and ate more cake. "But I like it. Just think about how many letters this thing has opened."

Barbara used the antique tool to slide open her own letter and pulled out the paper. "I've never seen anything written by my aunt." Eagerly, she started to read. The hand was liquid, dancing like waves over the paper, its curves and loops whispering of a forgotten love. When Barbara finished, she read the next letter, and the next.

When she looked up again, the bright light had turned into the soft glow of an early afternoon.

"What does she say?" Christy asked eventually. She had cleared the tea things and brought over a pitcher of iced lemonade and a plate of Agatha's light, buttery lemon cookies, lest they'd get hungry again. "Do you mind sharing? You don't have to, of course."

"But it would be nice," Agatha said quickly. "Since we *were* the ones who found the letters."

"It's like you said. Doris loved someone named James. She loved him very much," Barbara murmured.

"But?" Agatha had picked up on the hesitation in the words.

"But I don't remember anyone called James." Barbara cleared her throat. "I'm sure my mother would have mentioned him to me, wouldn't she? As far as I know, my aunt never married."

"Then your aunt had a secret boyfriend. Maybe that's why she moved into the cottage. Back in the day, there weren't too many single young ladies who had their own house." Agatha smiled.

"Well, she did live with my mother whenever my dad was traveling." Barbara tilted her head and laid down the letters. "It seems that James left Doris to join the war effort. His family came from Liverpool, and he felt obligated to fight for England. I guess he never came back. If he had, Doris would have given him the letters. Instead, she hid them in the wall."

Agatha cleared her throat twice. "Do you remember the old man who lived in this cottage when your parents sold it, Barb?"

"Of course. Jimmy. Jim, the hermit. Oh. Oh!" Barbara's eyes widened.

"That's exactly right." Agatha nodded slowly. "His name was Jim."

"James," Christy murmured. "Jim stands for James. Maybe James came back for his Doris after all."

Barbara stood. Suddenly, she didn't feel so good. Maybe it was all the whipped cream. Maybe not. Flustered, she gathered her aunt's love letters. "Ladies, thank you for the letters and the marvelous cake, and the—but now I think..." She drew a breath and managed a smile. "I think I should go home. I have to read these again."

CHAPTER 16

I don't understand." Barbara let go of the ruby-red rose with petals as soft as velvet. It fell back in its place, joining the other blooms in the rosebush. "I don't understand anything at all anymore."

"I'm sorry to hear that," Lukas murmured. "Would you like to have a few of those roses for the blue vase in the living room?"

"No. Lukas, I don't want to talk about flowers, or vases, or the house. Please." Barbara started walking down the sandy path that wound through the rose garden down to the sea.

"Would you like to be alone?"

She stopped. "Yes?" The word was not an affirmative, but a whole world of questions.

Lukas kept pace. "You're upset."

"So what?" She sighed. "What are you going to do about it, Luke? Feed me macarons?"

Unperturbed, he smiled. "Would you like macarons?"

"No, I don't want food. You know I don't." She smiled back and continued walking.

"I could call your friends," he suggested. "If you think that company would help."

"Not right now. In fact, I basically ran from them." Barbara ran a hand over the lavender. "I had to think."

"Should I leave?"

She looked up at him. "Stay."

Lukas stopped walking. "Why?" he asked in a low voice.

Barbara bent to rub a lavender blossom between her fingers and release the fragrance. "Why what?"

"Why should I stay? Why should I stay if you want to be alone?"

Barbara tilted her head. The sun glittered golden on the water, and the sea was as calm as a mirror. "I might want something."

He held her eyes. "What do you want, then? Not macarons or roses or friends."

"No, not those." She resumed walking. Earlier, Agatha had said that Barbara didn't need to pretend because she was rich. But sometimes, it was hard to say the truth anyway. Money helped tremendously. But it didn't fix everything. Not by far.

She inhaled a big breath of the aromatic air. "I don't want my friends. But I want company."

"You want..." He raised his eyebrows, prompting her to keep talking.

"I want *your* company, Luke." Barbara glanced over her shoulder at him. "There, I do. Is that okay?"

He nodded once. For a moment she thought he wasn't going to say anything. But then, a small smile tugged on the corner of his mouth. "Yes," he replied. "That's okay."

She pulled her sun hat lower. "I hope..." She cleared her throat. "I hope *everyone's* okay with that. Do you think?" She started walking, unable to look into his eyes.

Again, Lukas kept pace with her. "I'm certain everyone is okay with that." The smile had left his lips, settling on his vocal cords instead.

Barbara had never asked Lukas about his feelings for Margrit. She'd always figured that one day, the two of them would find each other. Yet it had never happened. At least not as far as she knew.

And sometimes, in the dark of the night, when Barbara lay alone in her big bed, her mind going over the day that had just passed, she wondered whether she wanted it to ever happen. Would she really be so pleased if the news came?

The sand turned into gravel, and instead of rose beds there now was only grass that rolled, soft and short and green, down to the sandy beach.

"Is there something on your mind?" Lukas asked after a while. "You know your thoughts are safe with me."

"Yes." She reached the cast iron bench by the cypress and stopped. "Sit with me. Please."

They sat, a good two hands of space between them.

"The thing is," she said after a short consideration. "I read all the letters my aunt wrote."

"Yes." He looked straight out at the sea. "You told me about your aunt and the cottage, and I remember."

"Well." She folded her hands. "By now I'm fairly sure that Jim was really her James, the man to whom she wrote her love letters. He did return and found out where she'd lived. I wish he had come earlier. And I wonder if Doris would still be with us if he had come back in time."

Lukas turned to study her face. "Do you think your aunt ended her life because she couldn't go on without him?"

Barbara shrugged her shoulders. "Loneliness can be tricky," she said. "But Doris was young, and my mother said she was resilient too. So I believe the shell seeker who saw Doris drown must have had it right. It was a rip tide that pulled her under, not loneliness. It's just...if Jim had been with her, maybe she wouldn't have gone swimming that day."

"And maybe she would have," Luke said gently. "We cannot know these things."

"I suppose we cannot." She pressed her lips together. The ocean was smooth today, beautiful and still. But it was an awesome force of nature, wild and free and untamable down to its very core. Human life meant no more to it than grass blades or rocks.

"There's something else on your mind. What is it?" Lukas propped his elbow on the armrest of the bench and put his chin in his hand, gazing out at the sea.

Barbara cleared her throat. "There's more in the letters, but I haven't told my friends," she admitted. "I want to look into it before I share."

"Can I help?"

"No. Well...maybe."

His smile was just visible. "Tell me."

"Okay." Barbara straightened her back. "It seems that Doris was pregnant when James left to join the war. Only, she didn't know it yet. The first few letters, she talked about always being tired. When the morning sickness settled in and she missed her period twice in a row, she caught on."

Lukas turned to her. "She was going to have his baby?"

Barbara nodded, gripping her hands together to calm her mind. "That's what she wrote in her letters. And yet..." She shook her head.

"And yet, as a child, you knew your aunt Doris. And you never saw her with a baby," Lukas completed her sentence when she didn't.

She heaved a tight breath. "How did you know?"

"You'd have told me. You never mentioned having cousins," he said simply. "I'm sure in my years here, I'd have heard about relatives if you had any."

"You're right again." As if the turmoil in her heart roused the wind, a breeze swirled over the water, rippling the surface. "I would have loved to have a cousin. Which leaves me with the disturbing question of...well."

"Where is the baby?" He asked the question on her behalf. "What happened to the baby?"

"Exactly. What happened? She must have been in a tight spot; she was young and unwed, and my grandparents were very strict indeed. I imagine she'd have confided in my mother; the two of them were so close. But I was close with my mother as well, and she never breathed a word about her sister's pregnancy. Did she have a miscarriage? Or do I have a secret cousin somewhere? I want to know. Even if the answer is difficult."

Lukas glanced her way, his eyes meeting hers. "Would you like me to make some inquiries in Mendocino? Someone might remember something."

"Inquiries?" She tipped her head to the side. Her gut reaction was a definite no. Let's not wake sleeping lions. Let's not stir the pot.

But her tongue wouldn't form the words.

How much longer was she going to be around? And when it was time to go, would she rather take with her the burden of open mysteries or difficult answers? "I suppose knowing the truth means living life to its fullest," she said after a while. "Most of my life is behind me. I intend to use the rest well."

"I'm with you." The look Lukas gave her was dark and soft and tempting, a portal that, if Barbara stepped through, could easily sink her into oblivion.

She breathed deeply, grounding herself, and turned her gaze back to the sea. Small waves had started to ruffle the calm water. They reared like foals from the water, their manes foaming white when they dove back into the sea. Streaks of wispy gray and lavender clouds reached across the sky.

The brim of her sun hat started to flap in the cool breeze. She took it off, absentmindedly kneading it in her hands. "Okay," she said. "Let me know if you find out something about a baby in the cottage. Let me know if you hear about old Jim too."

He gave a quick, affirmative nod. "I will also get us a copy of the sales records for the cottage. If Jim really was James, the name will be on there. We should start by making sure it's the same man to whom Doris wrote the letters." Lukas stood, offering Barbara a hand to help her up. She took it and rose. Against her expectation, he didn't move, staying where he was instead of stepping back to give her space.

Barbara looked up at him; she was closer to his face than she'd ever been before. His eyes were liquid and dark, a secret she suddenly felt needed exploring as much, if not more, as that of the missing baby.

"A storm is coming," he murmured and reached out to tuck a dancing curl of windblown silver behind her ear. "Take my arm. Let's leave before it arrives."

CHAPTER 17

The sinking sun embraced the rolling hills of the Mendocino vineyard, painting the sky in tangerine and lavender. In the warm air, the aroma of ripening grapes mingled with the scent of dry, golden grass, and the sounds of laughter and the clinking of glasses filled the vinery's terrace. The melodies of a Spanish guitar floated into a canopy of twinkling lanterns, each flickering like a firefly eager to join the celebration.

When Agatha had arrived, most of the seats were already taken. She swallowed her nervous excitement and joined the crowd on the lantern-lit terrace that was quickly becoming Mendocino Cove's go-to place for celebrations.

The long tables were covered with crisp white linens, colorful napkins, and vases full of golden-orange poppies. Dinner hadn't been served yet, but appetizer platters of freshly baked breads and artisanal cheeses, bowls overflowing with jewel-toned grapes and berries, and jars of wine and sparkling waters crowded the tables. From the kitchen inside, the scents and sounds of sizzling meat and grilled vegetables drifted over.

Agatha nervously shifted her weight. Ryan and his parents had promised to be here, but she couldn't find them. All the drive over her, she'd tried to think about what she could talk about that a thirteen-year-old boy was interested in. Not baking or renovating cottages. She didn't know the first thing about video games or computers and had never understood the rules of soccer. There were too many corners and lines and player positions. The relationship with her grandson was slipping through her fingers.

"Agatha! Over here!" Christy was waving, pointing to the empty chairs beside her.

Agatha wound her way past the other guests milling about to reach her friend. "I'm so glad you saved me a chair." She sat and nodded at Barbara, who was sitting on the other side of the table, sipping red wine.

"You look like three days of rain," Christy noted. "And it's such a beautiful night."

"Your family hasn't come yet," Barbara said softly and poured Agatha a glass of wine so rich and red it was almost black. "Have a glass. Have two if it cheers you up. Lukas will drive you and Christy home."

"But they're still coming," Agatha protested and lifted her glass to smell the liquid. It was fruity and smooth, evoking long summer walks over oak-covered hills. She tasted it. "Mmm," she said, surprised. "This is good."

Christy smiled and nodded in the direction where Jon, the vintner, was laughing with a group of friends. "He'll be delighted to hear it," she said. "But be careful. The wine is strong, and you're not used to drinking."

"Bah." Agatha emptied her glass, drinking in long, thirsty sips of the velvety red wine. "Aah. I needed that."

"Are you all right?" Christy patted Agatha's back before taking a piece of the soft sourdough bread and biting into it.

"Listen, everyone!" Jon was clapping his hands, and the guests fell silent. "All right, as you all know, we're here to celebrate my wife's ascension from adjunct to"—he took a deep breath and lifted Jenny's hand in the air as if she'd won first place in a race—"full on tenure-track professor!"

Jenny laughed and pulled her hand down while the guests cheered and clapped. "Thank you!" she called out and slipped her arm through her husband's. "It's no big deal in the big picture, but it means so much to me!"

"Teach those students!" someone yelled from the back, and several people laughed, including some, Agatha thought, who looked young enough to be Jenny's actual students.

"I intend to," Jenny promised. "I will teach them, and I will enjoy doing it. I will also research the history of our beloved town and let you all know if I find something interesting."

The crowd, more than ready to be amused, cheered again, and Jon led them into a toast. "To my Jenny," he said and lifted his glass. "Who is as beautiful as she is smart and as kind as she is strong. May she have a long and prosperous career full of good students and fascinating artifacts and get at least one grant to fulfill her tenure requirements!"

Everyone lifted their glass and said their good wishes, and then the guests sat down to enjoy the appetizers and laugh and drink until dinner came. The sun sank, the tangerine fire faded from the sky, and the first stars began to twinkle over the rolling hills of the vineyard.

Agatha checked her phone. She'd missed a text. Eagerly, she tapped on the screen, her eyes flying over the few lines her son, Bobby, had written. "Oh. They're not coming." She coughed. It felt like a stone was pressing on her chest.

"What? Why not?" Christy leaned over to read the text.

"Marlene, my daughter-in-law, isn't feeling well." Agatha tried not to sound too pathetically disappointed. "Bobby doesn't want to leave her alone. Ryan has asked for a sleepover with his friends." She stuffed her phone into her bag and pushed her glass to Barbara. "Another one, please."

Barbara refilled the glass, and Agatha drank. "Hmm."

"Here, have a piece of cheese." Christy took Agatha's plate and filled it with samples from the board: firm Manchego and aged gouda, olives, crackers with fig spread, thick slices of creamy brie, rolls of prosciutto, Italian salami, and honey-glazed pecans.

"Hello, piece of cheese." Despite missing her family, Agatha suddenly had to smile. One could only be so miserable, sitting on a beautiful terrace with friends who plied her with wine and cheeses. Agatha bit into a thick, creamy-white slice of Manchego. "Mmm. So soft and mild."

"What's that cheese made from?" Christy tried to find the label.

"It's a Spanish sheep's milk cheese." Barbara swirled her wine. "It's my favorite. Have it with the fresh walnuts and some fig spread, you two. The glazed pecans and cranberries are better with the brie."

"You should visit your son," Christy said. "And talk to him. Tell him that you'd like to see him and Ryan more often."

"I already did." Agatha put the corner of the velvety brie she'd been nibbling on back on the plate. "I don't want to do it again. They barely have enough time to do their jobs and drive Ryan to all his activities. I'm sure if they'd want to see more of me, they would."

Barbara leaned forward, her blue eyes shining in the light of the lanterns. "Do you think your daughter-in-law is really sick? Or did she just not want to come?"

For a moment, Agatha considered. Had Marlene and Bobby simply been too tired for the long, late drive and used a white lie to spare her feelings? "No," she decided. "She really must be sick. Bobby would just tell me if they didn't want to come. And I would understand. They're so busy."

"I wish they could move here." Barbara settled back.

"This is nothing. They are thinking about moving to Singapore," Agatha confided gloomily.

"Okay, let's not snowball; call your son tomorrow. Here comes dinner. Let's eat." Christy moved glasses and appetizer plates out of the way so the posse of hired teenage helpers could put down their dinner plates.

"Meat, fish, or vegetarian?" a girl with curly brown hair asked Agatha.

She did a quick scan of the table. Barbara already had the vegetarian option in front of her, and it looked like portobello mushrooms filled with quinoa, spinach, feta cheese, and herbs, while Christy had picked a lemon herb baked salmon.

"I'll take the meat, please," Agatha said, and the teen handed her a plate. "What is it?" She set the plate down in front of her.

"Slow-roasted lamb marinated in a blend of rosemary, garlic, and olive oil, with a red wine reduction and roasted vegetables. Enjoy." The girl hurried away to get more plates.

"Everybody, go ahead and eat, don't wait!" Jon called. "No point in letting Hannah's delicious food get cold! We have plenty of appetizers, and there's a dessert buffet, so nobody has to be hungry waiting until they're served."

"All right." Agatha refilled her own wine glass and picked up her fork and knife, scooping up a portion of the buttery soft roast. "It's very good," she reported. "Yummy."

"So's the salmon. Cheers, ladies." Christy put down her silverware and lifted her glass. "Agatha's getting twiddly already, so let's clink glasses while she can."

Barbara followed Christy's example. "Here's to your new cottage," she said. "And to friends moving to town.

And to Agatha, because she's the truest friend anyone can have. Including her family."

"And here's to you, Barbara, for being fabulously rich and sharing your wealth so generously," Christy added. "You have no idea how appreciative I am of your offer to drive us home."

Agatha just drank, and then they ate their delicious dinners, and when they were finished, they went to the dessert buffet together to fill their plates.

Jon and Jenny loved to entertain and knew how to make their guests happy. This time, they had laid out rows and rows of chocolate ganache cake, hazelnut praline éclairs with cream and glossy glaze, chocolate mousse with fresh raspberries, pistachio macarons with a hint of rose water in the luscious filling, delicate tartlets with tangy lemon curd and blueberries, and, Agatha's favorite, salted caramel cheesecake bites. She took a little of everything and also a bowl of vanilla ice cream, topped with freshly whipped cream and generously doused in hot raspberry sauce.

The music changed when the guitar player was called to have dinner himself, and a small band of musicians took his place. Soon the first guests got up to dance, and the team of servers, under Hannah's oversight, began to clear the tables and set out fresh glasses and clean dessert plates.

"Christy? I'm glad you're still here. I was hoping to catch you." Ethan appeared suddenly, dressed in a suit and tie that he was pulling loose. He smiled at Agatha and Barbara. "Good evening, everyone."

"Where have you been hiding?" Agatha demanded. She was a little fuzzy from the wine, though the rich food had done a lot to clear her head.

"I missed dinner; I just returned from a trip to San Francisco." He smiled wistfully and raked his fingers through his hair. "Wish I had left earlier. It smells amazing."

"I'm sure there's plenty left in the kitchen," Christy said. "You were looking for me?"

"I was." Ethan gave a quick, affirmative nod. "I thought I'd try asking you for a dance."

"Oh. Um. Sure." Christy rose and took the offered hand. "I'll see you later, girls," she said, and then Ethan led her onto the dance floor.

"Hmm." Barbara narrowed her eyes as she watched them dance. "I see."

"They used to date when they were rosy-cheeked babies," Agatha explained and picked up the napkin that had fallen from Christy's lap. She laid it on the chair, watching the laughing dancers. "I wish I had someone to dance with."

"You're very put-upon tonight," Barbara noted.

"Yeah. I am." Agatha emptied the last of her glass but held up her hand when Barbara offered to refill. "Nah. Thanks though, Barb."

"Barbara?" Another man had appeared. "Do you feel like dancing?"

"Thank you, Mitch, but not now. Go ask the lady over there. She's been tapping her foot all along."

"Okay. Catch you later." The man waved and disappeared back into the crowd.

"Well..." Barbara stood. As always, she was impeccably dressed, wearing an expensive wrap-dress in a deep burgundy, with plenty of understated diamond and gold jewelry. "I do want to swing a leg, but with you. May I ask for this dance?" She held out a hand.

Agatha pulled her chin back. "You want to dance with me? I'm wearing corduroy overalls and sneakers, Barb."

"I like it. Not for myself, but I like it for you. Because I like you, dear Agatha." Barbara walked around the table and took Agatha's hand, pulling her up.

"Okay." Agatha smiled, secretly pleased at the declaration of friendship.

The dance floor was full enough that nobody paid much attention to them. Despite her age, Barb was a great dancer, graceful and with a refreshing disregard for anyone's opinion on her form. Agatha relaxed, getting into the song. It was usually her who got her friend into situations, not the other way around. But maybe it was the wine, or the sweet, starlit night, but soon, Agatha forgot about her family and began to enjoy dancing with her friend.

"Watch this." Smiling, Barbara twirled Agatha around. She was surprisingly strong, and Agatha had to laugh. She was dizzy and warm, and the rhythm swept her away like a rising tide that pulsed in her veins. "Now you've got it!" Barbara called over the music and let Agatha go to dance a cha-cha step, her hands in the air. "Let's have fun while we're young!"

CHAPTER 18

The music changed into a softer, fuller song, and the dancing couple slowed down, wrapping their arms around each other and swaying to the melody. The night breeze played with Christy's hair, cooling her neck, and the soft glow of the lanterns and the full moon cast an ethereal light on the dance floor.

"Are you okay?" Ethan murmured, his low voice barely audible over the music that filled the starry night. "Are you getting tired?"

Apart from the fact that they'd danced together too long already, that she should leave right now, that this was turning into more than a dance at a lovely party... She drew in a long, slow breath. "I'm fine."

"I'm glad." He dipped his head to see her eyes, and his smile reached her soul and her heart at the same moment. Christy nestled deeper in the embrace of his strong yet gentle arms and closed her eyes. No man had made her feel like this before. No man other than Ethan, a hundred years back. Had she been waiting a lifetime to see him again?

Christy knew she shouldn't close her eyes like that. She should keep them open and her wits sharp, remembering the present, the facts, reality. But her head simply refused to fight her heart. And her body, instead of stepping back and putting a gap between them, still remembered the hands of her first lover. The fit of his arms, the warmth that enveloped her, his forgotten yet familiar scent transcended decades.

The song faded, giving way to an even sweeter, slower melody.

Ethan's hand pressed on the small of Christy's back, guiding her with a familiarity that conjured memories from when they were young. Poor art students wildly in love and newly released into the wild, they'd danced together through the Summer of Love in the bars of Haight-Ashbury. They'd danced like this—too close, too quiet—in the Fillmore Auditorium, the Avalon Ballroom, the Magna Cum Laude Coffeehouse, danced through the night and the laughter and the crowds. Christy had felt as safe in Ethan's arms as she'd felt safe in his love.

"I'm sorry," she whispered and laid her head on his shoulder, drinking in the familiar, intoxicating scent of his skin that was like home. "I'm sorry I thought you broke my heart when you kissed my sister."

His shoulder moved as he held her even closer. "I did break your heart."

A smile tugged on Christy's lips. "I'm starting to think I broke my own heart." She sighed, wondering what would have been had she been brave enough to stay and talk it out. It was so easy—and yet the hardest thing to do. "I was so scared. I didn't know it back then. But now I realize how scared I was."

"What were you scared of?" His lips moved against her hair.

Christy blinked. She hadn't had a lover in years. And even then, it had been an elegant, aloof affair, full of fancy dinners and texts and lipstick. Not the raw, emotional love she'd felt as a young student. But she'd been content. She had wanted her love affairs to be safe. She had wanted them to be distant, and elegant, and mostly in her head.

But now, her body remembered how it felt to be in love.

"What?" He slowed. "Do you want to sit down?"

"No. No. I just..." The sound that escaped her throat was half laughter, half sigh. "I don't want to sit. I want to dance forever. That's the problem."

He turned her, loosening his hold just enough so he could look at her face. "Why is it a problem, Christy?"

She shook her head. It was the last defense she had.

"Christy." He pulled her to him again, and his hand wandered lightly up her back until he gently guided her head to rest on his shoulder.

She couldn't resist the temptation to close her eyes again, letting him lead her into the steps of the dance.

"Tell me," he murmured. "Talk to me. You said you were scared. You say it's a problem to dance with me. And yet, you don't tell me why. Tell me why, darling."

Christy realized that they'd already crossed the last line she'd drawn between them. "I wasn't good enough.

I didn't deserve you. I didn't deserve love. Something in me broke when I realized."

"What broke?" he whispered. "None of it was true, but what broke?"

She blinked. "I thought it was my heart, but maybe it was something different. A...fence, a border. Something that had held back demons I didn't know I had." She angled her face to see whether he understood.

"Demons?" He frowned, shaking his head once.

"Anxiety. Depression. Impostor syndrome. Perfectionism. *Issues*." She smiled. "Thinking I didn't deserve your love released lots of issues. They galloped across my heart, their cloven hooves smashing it to bits. And there I was, without a lasso or whip, left to reign them back in. It took me many years."

He lowered his head, softly kissing her forehead. "You truly loved me," he murmured. "But you were so young still. I never realized the one or the other. I was also too young." The muscles in his arms tightened to steel as he pulled her close to him.

His kiss on her skin reverberated through her, sending sparks shivering down her spine. She had to inhale deeply before she could speak again. "Well, I've had forty years to learn how to reign the monsters back in. I forgive you."

The music changed again, and Ethan stopped dancing. Christy stepped away from him, leaving the warm safety of his arms so she could see him fully. The warm breeze whispered past them, carrying the soft silver light of the starry sky, the subtle scents of aged wine and sweet grapes, the insignificance of time.

"Christine."

"I'm here," she whispered. Meeting Ethan's eyes, Christy saw the reflection of their shared history—of their youthful love that had not weathered the storms of coming-of-age, the passion of hurt innocence. The lines etched on their faces told of separate journeys, years and decades that had humbled them and grown them, maturing their souls and hearts. But the look in his eyes—and the joy in her heart—also whispered something else to Christy. Under the full moon of a warm Mendocino night, their separate threads intertwined once again into the same story.

Christy rose on her tiptoes and, for a brief moment of eternity, pressed her lips to his. There was no more doubt in her heart.

Ethan took a shuddering breath and closed his eyes before looking down at her. "Really?" His low voice was almost a growl.

"What do you mean, really?" She smiled.

"You think you can kiss me like that?"

Christy tipped her head, feeling her smile deepen. "Like what?"

"So...casual." His arms encircled her, and he pulled her back to him. "And brief."

He was so close she had to tilt back her head to see his face. "Too casual?" she whispered, her eyes searching his. "Too brief?"

A deep, low sound came from his throat, and he lowered his head, closing the gap between them. His mouth brushed hers, an exploration that tasted of starlight and aged wine, of dancing and vineyard. It sent a tremor through Christy, a subtle quake she recognized in the depths of her being. She leaned her head further, offering herself to him, and heard him suck in air.

"Don't move like that, Christy. I'm not man enough to say no." His breath brushed her cheeks, her chin, her collarbone, and then his lips crushed hers with a hunger that had grown for decades.

With a small gasp, she broke away. "Ethan." She didn't know if she should laugh or cry or do anything at all.

He lowered his eyebrows, unrepentant. "Yes?"

"There are people around," she whispered and pressed a finger to her mouth. Already, her lips were swollen from the pressure of his mouth on hers.

"You're blushing." He smiled and reached out, trailing a finger down her cheek before he tucked a loose curl of hair behind her ear. "That was just a kiss."

She smiled back, quickly glancing at the dancers around them. But nobody was watching. "I'm not blushing," she murmured. "I'm much too old to blush because of a kiss. It's your stubble scratching me."

He laughed and rubbed a hand along his chin and jawline. "Come home with me, and I'll shave." He kissed the hand he was holding. "For you, I'll shave every day."

She tilted her head. "Every day?"

"Every day." He shook his head. "Every single darn day that I have left in this life, Christy."

"What if I leave the cove?" she whispered.

A shadow brushed over his face, so briefly she almost missed it. Then he started dancing again, effortlessly leading her with him. "This time, I'll come after you," he murmured, holding her eyes. "There's nowhere to run where I won't find you."

"Are you threatening me?" She smiled.

"Yes." He bent down and kissed her cheek. "The next time we have a misunderstanding, or a fight, or a problem, I will sit in your yard with my tape recorder, playing our music until you forgive me."

She chuckled and pulled her hand from his to circle his neck with her arms. "Or you could just call," she whispered. "We'll talk."

"No." His lips moved against her ear. "I recently found out that that's not good enough for me. I want to see you. I want to *touch* you." His fingers traced gentle circles on her lower back as he drew her closer.

Taking a calming breath, filling her lungs deeply, Christy let go of him and stepped away.

"Come back," he growled.

She shook her head. "What are we doing?" she whispered. "Two retirees, making out on the dance floor? We're not twenty again, and this is not the Fillmore Auditorium." She looked over her shoulder. Luckily, people were still too busy laughing and kissing and dancing themselves.

Ethan ran both hands through his hair. "Would you like to take a walk? The vineyard is beautiful."

"No." She laughed quietly. "Ethan, I came with my friends. I'm not going to walk off into the sunset all of a sudden." She turned back at him. "Agatha already feels lonely, and Barbara doesn't know very many people here. I'll stay and keep them company."

For a long while, he looked at her. Then he smiled, his blue eyes softening. "Of course." He took her hand and kissed it. "You are my queen, Christy," he murmured. "You always have been."

"Well then, your queen wants a glass of cool water and your secret phone number." She pulled her hand away only to slip her arm under his. "And she wants you to dance with someone else because otherwise I'll start making out with you on the dance floor. Nobody wants to see that."

"You're wrong about that." He laughed quietly, leading her back to her table. "*I* want to see that. All night long, from every angle." He let her go to pull out her chair.

"Hush!" Now she really was blushing, but at least nobody had heard. She sat, and Ethan poured her a glass of water. "Thank you."

"You're welcome." He put a hand on the back of the chair and leaned over her. "Now that I've found you again, I'll do whatever it takes to stay in your life," he murmured, suddenly serious. "I will never kiss you again if you don't want me to kiss you. I'll never come around unless you want to see me. I want all of you, but if talking on the phone is all you're ready to give, I'll take it. Just...don't disappear from my life like last time. I've searched for you ever since, even if I didn't know it. But I can't do it again. I'll crack, and my demons won't only gallop over my heart but eat me alive. So promise. Out of pity, out of mercy, I don't care. Just promise me."

Christy reached up with one hand, cradling his face to ease the storm in his eyes. "Yes, I promise you," she whispered. "We're going much too fast. But I promise."

"We'll slow down, if you want." He rose and straightened his shoulders, exhaling a long, tight breath. "Call me?"

"I will. Soon." Her heart beating, Christy watched him walk away.

He didn't look back, but he also didn't ask any other woman to dance; he left the party and crossed the silver-dipped parking lot, got in his car, and drove away.

When Christy turned back to the table, Agatha and Barbara stood before her.

"Well well well," Agatha said, grinning widely. "I believe you've just secured yourself a free architect for your renovations."

"Oh, Agatha!" Christy started laughing as all the tension that had wound up her heart and her lungs started to unravel like a tense rubber band that had suddenly snapped free. "You're terrible."

Her friends took the empty chairs on either side of Christy. Someone poured cool, golden wine in fresh crystal glasses, and a server slid a tray of caramelized onion and goat cheese tartlets, citrus-marinated shrimp skewers, and prosciutto-wrapped figs in front of them.

"Right." Barbara helped herself to a tartlet and a glass. "Spill. You two were practically making out on the dance floor. What did he say to you? We want to know everything."

CHAPTER 19

Years and years ago, before phones and computers, Christy had owned a record player. It had been one of her most treasured possessions. Red and shining, its little diamond needle had teased all her favorite songs from the LPs she collected. Unfortunately, it had gone the way of all electronics and played its last tune a long time ago.

Wistfully, she looked through the stacked LPs in the old banana box, pulling out covers that caught her eye or reminded her of past favorites.

The vendor, a young man with John Lennon glasses—or maybe now they were Harry Potter glasses, Christy wasn't sure—tossed his glossy hair back. "See anything you like?"

She shook her head. "I used to have a collection. Now I don't even have a record player."

The young man pushed his hands into his pockets. "Got to get one again. Kids these days want books and all that in their life, just the way it used to be. You can buy record players everywhere, not just at flea markets." He coughed thoughtfully. "Though you can probably find one around here."

"I'll have a look. If I find one, I'll come back and buy some of your records." She waved and strolled to the next colorful stall. It offered knickknacks, vintage fashion jewelry, and crocheted baby blankets in cotton-candy pink and blue. Christy bought a small white cat figurine Agatha would like for her mantle, chatted a few words with the seller, and walked on. The air smelled of vintage treasures and street food.

Suddenly starving, she stopped by the nearest cart and bought a slice of halloumi. It was grilled to perfection, and the smoky, savory cheese melted in her mouth. Wiping her mouth with a paper napkin, she smiled. "That was so good."

The young woman in the food truck smiled back. "Try my grilled elote. It's corn on the cob slathered with a spicy mayo and sprinkled with cotija cheese and chili powder. It's just as smoky as the cheese you just had."

"I'll keep it in mind for later. Thanks." Christy put a tip into the jar and wandered on, thinking that she would buy an LP after all. She couldn't forget the one she'd loved as a student.

She turned back. As she passed a display of silk scarves, her gaze unexpectedly locked on to a familiar face. Ethan! He was browsing her banana box of vinyl records, fully absorbed in his own little world. A surge of excitement danced through her veins. After the party at the vineyard, she'd felt like she needed to slow things down—this time, she was not going to wildly fall head over heels for him. That felt too much like a repeat of their first relationship. This time, she wanted to build things nice and slow and solid.

"Ethan?" she called out.

He turned toward her, his eyes widening in surprise before breaking into a warm smile. "Christy!" He went to greet her, taking her hand into his own. "I was hoping to run into you here. It's been two days." He looked for permission in her eyes, then leaned down and kissed her cheek. "You look stunning. How are you?"

"Very good." She smiled at him. "I see you found the stall with the old records." Nodding at the woven shopping bag hanging on his shoulder that showed a distinctly square shape, she asked, "Did you buy any?"

"This? No." He lifted the bag and opened it. "This is something else. In fact, it's a watercolor. I found it buried under a pile of vintage superman comics."

She tilted her head. "Watercolor? Aquarelles are my specialty." She stopped herself and laughed, embarrassed. "I should get used to saying, *used to be* my specialty. I already feel out of the loop."

"Nonsense. Once an expert, always an expert." He pulled the painting out of the bag. "I like the frame."

Christy took the painting from him, her eyes scanning it out of habit. It was beautiful, a seascape in varied greens and blues, full of life and energy. The composition lifted her spirit without effort. She smiled as she moved the painting so the sun could lighten up different aspects. The colors were lighthearted, interesting, not calling attention to themselves but supporting the general mood in a very—Christy blinked and lowered the frame. "I like the frame too. And the painting. It's pretty." She held it out for Ethan. "Make sure you don't damage it in that thin bag."

Calmly he took it, stowing it out of sight again. "Christy, I don't know if it's all right to ask a favor."

"Um." Her smile dried up. She couldn't very well say no to returning the favors he had done her, but she had a feeling that his wishes would lead her onto swampy grounds indeed. She was done with paintings and all that. She took a breath. "You can always ask." It sounded even more ungracious than she'd meant to.

He smiled, unbothered. "I was wondering if you would have a close professional look at it for me. I've got a feeling that a significant artist did it. You could help me find out."

She shook her head. Not because of the painting, but because she wasn't doing appraisals.

"I'll widen the upstairs window for you. It's the last thing you want done to finish the cottage, isn't it?" His smile deepened. "Come on. Strike a deal with an old hippie, huh? How can you refuse?"

Finally, she cracked and smiled back. "Old hippie indeed. Is that suit from the Italian designer I think it is?"

"Yes." He ran a hand through his hair, perfectly at ease about showing up to a flea market in clothes that cost more than all the stalls on this street combined. "I met a friend for lunch at the restaurant. Otherwise I'd also be in jeans and a T-shirt now. Which, by the way, suits you very much."

"Ha." Christy hooked her arm under his, and they started walking. "The upstairs window in the bedroom?"

"That's the one. Wouldn't it be nice to lie in bed, looking out at the rolling waves at night?"

Christy chuckled. No—the sound was too high and rapid to be a chuckle. She was *giggling*. She took a slow, deep breath to tame the teenage silliness tickling in her throat. "All right. I'll bite. A window for a picture."

"Fabulous." He held out the bag with the picture. "Here you go."

"Oh. Okay." She angled her body to take it, reaching across him.

Laughing, he kissed the top of her head and slung the bag back over his own shoulder. "Gotcha. You really thought I'd make you carry it, didn't you?"

"Yeah. Ha. Funny." She shook her head but had to laugh too at the little trap he'd laid.

Ethan stopped at a food cart. A sweet and warm fragrance that was impossible to resist wafted from it. "How do you feel about churros? It's been ages since I tried them last."

"I feel great about them. Actually, I was just looking for dessert when..."

"When you found me. I'm your dessert, don't you know?" He waggled his eyebrows.

"Oh goodness." Again, she had to laugh. "Stop, seriously."

"All right." Ethan bought them two churros, handing her one of the thick, deep-fried dough pastries that were generously coated in cinnamon sugar and wrapped in wax paper. "Here you go."

"Thank you." Christy tasted her treat, and it was all she'd hoped for. Sweet, decadent, deep-fried. Eating their treats, they wandered on, stopping at the stalls to admire self-made sea-glass jewelry, hand-carved wooden turtles and felt gnomes, tie-dyed shirts, mega-packs of cheap socks, and the usual vintage knick-knacks any flea market worth their salt offered.

"Well, look here." Ethan pointed at a brass circle peeking out from behind a table. "Is that a gramo-phone?"

"Yup." The seller, a large man in his seventies, nod-ded. "It sat in my shed all these years, so I don't know if it still plays." With an almighty groan and considerable difficulty, he lifted the gramophone on the table.

"Was it kept dry?" Ethan asked, running a hand over the beautiful horn. When he looked at his fingers, they were full of dust.

"Yep. Dry as all dickens. Tell you what. I don't want to take this thing back again. It takes up too much space in my car, and I'd rather give my friends a ride to the old pub, if you know what I mean."

"I think I do." Ethan pulled out a napkin and cleaned his hand. "How much do you want?"

"Fifteen." The seller held out a hand as large and white as a flounder.

Ethan pursed his lips and looked at Christy. Smiling, she shrugged. "I can't help you, Ethan. I've never used a gramophone in my life."

"Would you like to see if we can get this one to work?"

"It's romantic, isn't it? But it does take up a lot of space."

"Space I have."

"Ten," the seller said and lifted his hand.

"Done." Ethan shook. "For the heck of it."

"That's right." The seller took the ten-dollar bill Ethan handed him and grinned. "That's exactly right."

Ethan lifted the gramophone and, best as he could, tucked it under his arm. "I think that's it for me," he said to Christy as they walked on. "Unless you'd like to pick out some of those LPs. We'll need something to play on this."

"If you can get it to work." *We*, he'd said. *We'*ll need something to play on it.

They picked out a few records from bands they both had liked back in the days, and Christy helped Ethan bring everything to his car and stow it away. Then Ethan closed the trunk and leaned against it.

"I meant to ask," he said, his eyes searching her face. "Have you called your nieces yet?"

Christy nodded. "I called," she said and crossed her arms, hugging herself as if it weren't a perfectly sunny and dry day. "I left a message on the answering machine. But I haven't heard back." She looked at the ground. Her tennis shoes were dusty from the street. "I'm not surprised. We haven't been in touch for too long. I don't expect they're very excited to hear from me."

"You're their aunt," he said gently. "Let's give it a little longer."

"Yeah." She smiled up at him, suddenly uncertain. "I'm trying not to expect anything. They have a right to hate me. I should have been there for Abby and them, and I wasn't. I failed them rather spectacularly."

"They don't hate you." His voice was gentle. "Hey. I don't know them well, but I do know them a little bit. They don't hate you. That's not who they are."

"Ah." She squinted against the sun shining in her eyes. "That's good to hear."

He sighed. "Can I see you tonight?"

"Tonight?" Agatha was going to make dinner, lemon soup with egg and—

"I can't forget kissing you," he said quietly. "I think we should talk."

"Talk?" Her heart started to flutter.

"Kiss, ideally." A smile tugged at the corners of his mouth. "But I'll settle for talking."

Agatha's lemon soup could possibly wait an hour or two... "Okay," Christy said softly. The memory of the kiss, his arms, the words they'd whispered suddenly lowered like a veil that made it impossible to think clearly.

"I can hardly think straight anymore, Christy, and I'm not used to that." His voice was low and hoarse. "I can't pretend we're nothing but friends."

She traced the outline of her lips with her fingertip, lost in thought.

"You have to stop doing that," he said softly, taking a step closer to her.

"Sorry." She dropped her finger and tipped her head to look into his face. "I'll see you at five?"

He exhaled. "Five at the cottage?"

"Five at the cottage," she confirmed. She took the bag with the painting from him and slung it over her shoulder, then stepped backward, pushing her hands into the pockets of her jeans.

His lips formed words he didn't speak.

She smiled and took another step away from him. "Don't forget to bring the gramophone and the records."

He shook his head. She turned and walked away, feeling his eyes on her until she dove back into the crowd at the flea market, losing her way almost as quickly as she'd once again lost her heart.

CHAPTER 20

So she said—" Agatha dipped a spoon into her soup and tasted it before finishing her sentence. "Yum!"

"Let me try." Christy shifted the cat to her other arm to take a fresh spoon from the drawer and taste the soup as well. "Avgolemono is a favorite of mine." The traditional Greek soup made of chicken stock, lemons, and eggs, had a velvety texture and a bright, citrusy flavor. "Mmm. It's really good, Agatha."

"I'll put some for you in the fridge," Agatha promised. "I also have bread in the oven and a bunch of seafood."

"No wonder it smells so good. Ethan had better take me somewhere nice." Christy lowered her spoon. "I'm sorry about leaving you hanging tonight."

"Don't be." Agatha carefully put the lid on the soup pot and turned off the flame. "Turns out I'll have visitors myself." A light danced in her eyes when she looked up.

"Really?" Christy rinsed her spoon in the spotless sink. "Who's coming over?"

"My son!" Agatha smiled widely, her entire face lightening up. "And he's bringing Ryan as well, and maybe Marlene is coming too. Maybe they're all coming."

"That's fabulous." Christy couldn't help but smile, happy that Agatha would have the company she liked best in the whole world tonight—that of her own family. "I'm so glad they're making time to get together."

"Me too." Agatha twirled her spoon between her fingers, restless. "Only, I'm a little worried."

"About?"

Agatha spread her hands in question. "What if they have news? Bobby sounded like he had something he wanted to talk about."

"Well, did you ask him?"

"No." Agatha looked up through her lashes. "I was scared. Scared that he..." She took a deep breath. "For crying out loud. I'm scared he got an offer for Singapore. What if they're leaving altogether?"

Christy didn't know what to say. The job in Singapore had been in the talks for a while now. Maybe it would come, maybe it wouldn't, Agatha had confided. But if the offer did come, it was sure to be too good to say no. A substantial increase in salary, a house, a car and driver on the dime of the company, and a bilingual, international upbringing for Ryan.

"Maybe it's something else," Christy murmured. She wanted to hug Agatha, help take the uncertainty out of what was to come. "Let's not assume the worst."

"If they leave the country now..." Agatha looked up, a piteous expression in her eyes. "Who knows if I'll see them again?"

Christy felt her own eyes widen. "Agatha, stop that right now! You don't even know what your son has to say!" Blowing awkwardness into the wind, she reached out and pulled her friend into a warm embrace. "You don't even know if they have *anything* to say," she whispered. Agatha smelled of soup, and the strawberry hair shampoo in the tiny bathroom, and the salty sea. "Maybe they just want to have a nice dinner with you."

Agatha sighed, then wiggled out of Christy's arms. "There's something," she declared. "I have to wait and see what it is."

"Just...remember that I'm here too," Christy said. "I'm your neighbor now. You won't be alone."

"No, I know." Agatha cleared her throat and tried a smile. It wasn't a very good smile, but the corners of her lips lifted up all right.

"I want to hear everything about it the minute they leave," Christy said bracingly. "All right?"

"Hmm." Agatha shook her head. "So Ethan is coming over, huh?"

"Yes. He promised he'd widen the upstairs window for me if I had a look at this painting he bought at the flea market."

"Oh! Back at it, are you?" The corners of Agatha's lips lifted higher. "I knew they couldn't keep you away for long."

"No, nothing like that." Christy raised an eyebrow. "I mean to say, I'm not back at it at all. The painting will turn out to be done by a talented local artist, nothing more."

"Okay. Calm down," Agatha said mildly and glanced at the large clock over the shelf with cooking books.

"You'd better go. Are you staying at your place for the night?"

"Well, the mattress came today. But I still don't have a bed frame," Christy said distractedly, smoothing her new linen dress and straightening the soft cardigan that went with it. Was it too nice for the evening? Not nice enough? She'd not dated in so many years; she had no idea how things were done these days.

"Who needs a bed frame?" The tentative smile had turned into a grin. "You look fabulous. For sure good enough to fix a window. Go. Don't make him wait."

"Okay." Christy shook her hair back. She did have butterflies in her stomach. "Good luck with your family tonight."

Agatha flicked her wrist in the direction of the door. "Yeah. You too."

Christy left her friend's house, grabbing her bag packed with necessities like a nightgown and a toothbrush, on the way out. Earlier, Jon and his cousin, Lex, had kindly carried her new mattress upstairs and put it under the window that still needed widening. They had also, very sweetly and without prompting, placed a few other pieces of furniture.

Her beloved desk from a library in San Francisco was in the room that would double as her office. Her sofa had arrived, and the only chair she'd ever liked, the antique copper coat stand and the art deco entrance table, as well as a small handful of dressers and armoires that were now in the two guest bedrooms upstairs.

All that was left was to buy a bed frame to fit her new mattress, unpack the last boxes, and stock the freshly painted pantry, the cabinets, and the new fridge with groceries.

The sun was sinking toward the sea when she stepped outside and pulled the door to Agatha's cottage closed behind her. The short walk in the mild, warm air was pleasant, and she picked a few wildflowers from the side of the street in passing. They would add a nice, bright touch to her kitchen.

Before she reached her own property, Ethan's car pulled up to the curb in front of it.

Smiling, she waited for him to get out and meet her.

He was wearing not a designer suit this time but the announced jeans and a white button-up with rolled-up sleeves. When he reached her, he kissed her cheek. "Good evening," he said. "I brought food."

"Did you really?" She'd expected he would take her out. But this was even better—the first dinner in the new house.

He pointed over his shoulder at his car. "You go ahead, I'll get the food. Oh, and the gramophone. I didn't forget."

"I'll help you," she decided and followed him to his car. Unlike his showy house, his car was a small sedan, a little old, a little beat up. But she liked it. It told her that Ethan didn't need to show off the money he had.

"Here." He handed her two white plastic bags with the logo of the local restaurant.

Crammed with Styrofoam containers, the bag felt warm to the touch and smelled scrumptious. "What do we get?" She inhaled the scent, a mix of charcoal grill and citrusy marinade, garlic and roast onions.

"It's surf 'n turf, specially ordered from the Mermaid Galley." He lifted the bulky gramophone from the trunk.

"You shouldn't have." Suddenly, Christy was starving.

"I absolutely should have. I don't do hungry." He winked at her. "Stick with me if you want to eat well, babe."

They went to the door, and for the first time, Christy unlocked her cottage in the knowledge that a cozy interior waited for them, not a chaos of boxes and crumpled newspapers and out-of-place furniture.

"It's beautiful," Ethan said as he followed her through to the kitchen. "I might be mistaken, but those gorgeous rugs are worth a kingdom, aren't they?"

"From Egypt," she agreed, keeping herself from launching into the adventurous story of how she'd acquired the antique beauties. "But they're real rugs, to walk on." She set her bags on the kitchen table and turned to look at him.

He nodded at the gramophone in his arms. "Where do you want this?"

"Here." She hurried to shift a stack of art magazines on a small table. "Does it work?"

"I cleaned the dust off, but I haven't tried it yet." He turned to take her hands. "How about we eat while the food is still hot? I got us a nice shrimp cocktail, grilled filet mignon with herb butter, broiled lobster tails, garlic mashed potatoes, and erm...right. Roasted asparagus. And I made the tiramisu for dessert. There's also a bottle of wine in one of those bags."

"That sounds lovely." Christy pulled dishes from her cabinet—first time—and set the table, then rummaged around for silverware. She'd forgotten what drawer she'd put them in. Laughing, Ethan helped her search, and eventually, the table was set.

"I need another vase," she said suddenly, remembering that all the vases she'd brought were filled and scattered throughout the house. "I picked these flowers walking over here, and they're already starting to wilt."

"How about a water glass?"

Christy lowered her chin. "My eighteenth-century crystal? Oh, I know. I saw a vase in the shed, where Jim kept his art supplies."

"Should I check?"

"I'll come with you." She opened the kitchen door to the warm, blue, coastal evening, and they both stepped out onto the small stone patio Christy had unearthed from under the weeds. The shed was only a few steps away, and soon, Ethan opened the creaking wooden door.

"Where did you see the vase?" he asked, letting her pass.

"Um." Inside the tiny shed, Christy turned around, breathing in the air that still smelled faintly of turpentine and pottery clay and cracking oil paint. "There. It's just sitting on that chest there."

"I see it." Ethan climbed over a stack of easels and tripods to get to the old, frayed chest made of woven reed and brass and picked up the vase. "Wonder what's in here." Carefully, he opened the lid and peeked inside. "Hey. Are those documents?"

CHAPTER 21

"H ello, Mom." Agatha's son, Bobby, kissed her cheek. "How are you?"

"I'm very well, thank you." Agatha patted her son's cheek and opened her arms, hoping Ryan wouldn't mind a hug.

"Hey, Grandma." The young teenager accepted the hug, awkwardly patting her back. "How are you?"

"Good, sweetheart. I'm real good, now that you're here."

"Hello, Agatha." Marlene, Bobby's wife, leaned across her son to kiss Agatha's cheek. "It's good to see you again. It's been too long."

Agatha let Ryan go, and the boy, relieved that part was over, straightened his T-shirt. "I'm just glad you could make time," she said, making the words sound bright and happy. They didn't need to know how much she'd wanted this visit to happen; knowing how lonely Agatha often was for their company would only be another burden they didn't need. "Come in. Come in. I made dinner."

"That sounds great, Mom." Bobby ushered his wife and son ahead of him into the cottage.

Agatha stayed a moment before she followed. She inhaled the floral evening air, bracing herself for what was to come. Whatever it was, she had to accept it with good grace. She wouldn't stand in the way of their best life. Maybe she'd even visit them in Singapore, though the flight was terribly long. She'd looked it up on the computer.

But for now, she would just enjoy their time together as much as she could. The moment of togetherness and connection might have to last her for months. Maybe even years.

"Are you coming, Mom?" Bobby called out.

Agatha closed the door. "Yes! I'm coming." She took a last deep breath, and then she went through to the kitchen.

Marlene was setting a box on the table. "I brought you a lemon cake," she said over her shoulder. "I know how much you enjoy them, and I made it from the recipe you gave me. I want to know what you think about it."

"That's so nice of you, sweetheart. Thank you." Agatha didn't need a lemon cake; her pantry was full of them. But her heart was touched because Marlene had a busy job as a phlebotomist and rarely found the time to bake.

"Of course." Marlene smiled, looking pleased.

"I thought we could eat on the patio," Agatha said, swallowing the fear that they were all extra-nice tonight in order to soften the blow that was about to come. "It's such a lovely evening. And I bought a soccer ball for Ryan." She turned to her grandson. "Maybe you can show me your soccer skills."

Ryan glanced at his dad, and Bobby's eyebrows rose. "Sure," Ryan said. "I can show you a trick I learned. It's like a sidestep that makes it look like I walk on air. It's cool."

Agatha smiled and opened the fridge. "Can't wait to see it," she said cheerfully. "Maybe you'll teach me how to do it myself."

"Yeah," he said doubtfully. "Maybe. You have to be kind of loose in the joints, though." He lifted his knee and shook his foot to demonstrate.

"I'm loose. Just you wait and see, baby." Agatha handed Bobby a tray with glasses and a pitcher of iced lemonade. "Would you bring that outside?"

Everyone pitched in carrying as they made their way to the patio. It really was lovely outside. Going on six o'clock, the sky wore bands of precious metals, and the rippling sea, pulling away from the land, reflected the glow, looking like molten lava. The mellow evening air smelled sweetly of roses and the kelp drying in the nearby rock pools.

With a pang, Agatha remembered that when he was little, Ryan had spent hours exploring them, hunting for crabs and sea stars, urchins and anemones. Now he only glanced at them in passing. It was a pity that her only grandchild couldn't grow up by the sea.

"You made soup?" Bobby sat and inhaled deeply. "It smells delicious."

"And it tastes even better." Agatha ladled the velvety avgolemono into deep bowls while Marlene broke the freshly baked bread and handed out large, steaming chunks of it.

They ate the creamy soup while Bobby and Marlene caught Agatha up on their life. Their stories, once again, made it clear that their life was hectic, crammed full of appointments and deadlines, school games and soccer practices, with little time to relax.

When the soup was gone, Agatha stood. "I made a seafood boil," she said, winking at Bobby. He'd always loved tackling the enormous steaming platters of mixed seafood.

"Really? Thank you." Bobby smiled back, and for a moment, a spark lit in Agatha's heart. Because there was nothing written in her son's brown eyes about leaving the country. On the contrary. A happy promise in his kind, soft irises seemed to be waiting for the right moment. But maybe it was just her imagination.

Agatha hurried into the kitchen, heart beating with a hope she didn't really want, in case it would get crushed later. From the oven, she pulled her large enamel-coated pan. It was piping hot and loaded with luscious lemon herb shrimp, plump garlic butter scallops, steamed crabs, boiled mussels, and three ruby-red lobsters—one for each of her guests. Trying not to spill the fragrant garlic wine sauce, she lifted it up and sat it on top of the stove when Marlene came into the kitchen, a stack of soup bowls in her hand.

"I'll swap these for plates." Marlene blinked a few times, and then she put a hand over her mouth and coughed.

"What's the matter?" Agatha cast a glance over her daughter-in-law as she pulled out another set of crocheted potholders from a drawer. There was another hot tray waiting in the oven, this one with baby potatoes tossed in olive oil, garlic, and herbs, then roasted until golden and crispy.

"Nothing! Nothing." Marlene's throat moved as she swallowed. "You go on ahead. I'll be right behind you with the plates; I'll just take a moment to powder my nose. Won't be a minute."

"All right, take your time. Plates are in the cabinet to the left." Agatha carried the seafood outside, wondering what was up with her daughter-in-law. Maybe the constant stress was finally getting to her, and she needed a moment to decompress. Sometimes, locking oneself into a bathroom was the only break one could get.

CHAPTER 22

I s your wife okay?" Agatha whispered to Bobby as he helped her set the heavy tray on the table.

A twinkle danced in his eyes as he smiled. "She's got a lot going on at work," he replied. Then he called out to his son, who was on the grass kicking the new ball.

"Here are the plates." Marlene came out, her face still glowing with the cold water she'd patted on her cheeks and neck.

"Are you sure you feel fine?" Agatha demanded, her eyes following a droplet running down Marlene's skin. "Here, sit down. What's going on?"

A smile of understanding passed between them. "Tell her, honey." Marlene sat down beside Bobby, and he took her hand into his. "Marlene is pregnant," he announced. "Ryan is going to get a sister in the fall. We're having a baby girl."

Agatha felt her jaw drop. "A baby girl?" she whispered and clutched her hands to her heart. "Really, Marlene?"

Marlene smiled and held out a hand for Agatha, who took it and squeezed it. "Yes, really. It was a surprise when I found out, let me tell you. And it seems I'm almost four months along too! We were thinking about calling her Lindsey, after my mom, and Agatha, after you. What do you think?"

"Little Lindsey Agatha?" Agatha pulled in a deep breath, feeling excitement flood her bloodstream. "I'm so happy I don't know what to say. Congratulations, darlings!"

"Thank you, Mom. Like Marlene said, it was a big surprise, but now we're both over the moon. There's more too. But let's start eating; this is too beautiful to let it go cold." Bobby called Ryan to the table, and once they were all seated and helped, he lifted his glass of lemonade.

"Here's to the health of Ryan and his sister!"

"How do you feel about it, Ryan?" Agatha asked.

Ryan suddenly broke into a grin. "I've always wanted a sibling," he announced. "I can't wait to have a sister."

They clinked their glasses and drank. Agatha couldn't wrap her mind around another grandchild, but it was the best possible news. Now she understood the happy little twinkle in her son's eyes she'd spotted earlier.

Bobby set down his glass and sampled the shrimp. "Mom—there's something else we want to talk about with you."

No! the word hurled through Agatha's mind like a cannonball. She lowered her fork. *Don't tell me you're leaving for Asia. Not now, not with little Lindsey. She'll never know me.*

"The thing is, Mom..." Bobby cleared his throat. "It's getting too much for Marlene and me where we are. Everything's spread out enough that we're still constantly in our cars. We make ends meet, but that's about it too." He cleared his throat. "I brought it up with my boss, and it seems that I can expect a big promotion. More responsibility, but more money too. If I take it, it would help us out a lot." He smiled at his wife. "Marlene could stop working and stay home with the baby if she wants."

"I'd like to. I'd really like to do that this time around." Marlene smiled.

"I understand," Agatha said quietly. Her appetite for mussels in white wine sauce was gone. "Of course then you must accept the offer."

"That's what I told him." Marlene smiled and leaned forward, putting her hand on Agatha's. "And what Bobby's trying to say is that the promotion will come with an option to work remotely. He'd only go in to see his team once or twice a week."

"Not Singapore?"

"Singapore?" Marlene looked surprised. "No, they hired someone new for that branch. Bobby, didn't you tell her?"

"I don't... I guess not." Her son shuffled his spoon around. "Sorry, Mom, it fell through the cracks. We had a lot going on with finding out about the baby and all that."

Slowly, Agatha lifted the mussel and cracked it open. Chewing, she looked from Bobby to Marlene and back. "But remote is good, isn't it? What's the catch?"

"The catch is that we're thinking of moving to Mendocino Cove," Marlene said. "So Bobby's commute for those days would be quite long. And Ryan would have to change schools."

"Aw man," Ryan muttered, but when Agatha looked at her grandson, he shrugged. "I guess I still know kids here, Grandma," he said. "Olli goes here. And Kyle. They're cool."

"And, of course..." Marlene cleared her throat. "Childcare would be a problem if I did decide to work part-time. There's no preschool here."

"I'll help with the baby," Agatha said quickly. "I'll take her, and she can play with Faye's little one. I'm sure there'll be another baby or two by November. I'll organize play dates, Marlene."

"I was hoping you would say that." Marlene smiled. "But wouldn't that be too much? It's a lot of work, watching babies."

"I'd *love* to do it. I know not everyone does, but I do." Agatha slumped back. "I *want* to be in my grandchildren's lives. Not as a bystander, but as a Grandma who helps raise them."

"Really, Mom? Even just taking a baby for a morning is a lot of work. And you're used to being by yourself," Bobby said, but she could tell he was only teasing her.

Agatha shook her head. "Maybe I'm used to being by myself," she said. "But I miss you and your family every day. I'd love to have you live in town, and I'd love to help with the kids."

"I didn't know you felt lonely, Mom. You never said." Bobby exchanged a glance with his wife.

"I couldn't very well tell you, could I?" Agatha spread her hands. "And I probably should've kept my mouth shut now too. You had to live your life, Bobby."

"You're part of my life, Mom." Bobby frowned. "And I'm glad you told me. If that's how you feel, then—"

"Then I suppose we'll start looking at houses a little bit earlier than planned." Marlene turned to the sea. "We won't be able to afford a cottage by the sea, but I'm sure there are other beautiful places. And I could possibly find something at the local hospital to help."

"Well," Bobby said complacently. "Let's see how much of a promotion it is. Maybe we can find a fix-er-upper at the sea after all."

Agatha felt like she was floating. She would have her family around her, her grandkids growing up around her, being at home in her very house and garden. She would be able to read dinosaur books to her little granddaughter and teach Ryan how to bake lemon tarts, show the kids where to find the best sand dollars and how to count the stars in the sky at night.

"I'm sure you can find a nice house," Agatha said, trying to keep her voice steady. "I'll ask around, shall I?"

Marlene helped Ryan to another crab and leaned back with a smile, a hand on the belly hiding under her wide shirt. "That would be fantastic, Agatha," she admitted. "I'd rather get started sooner than later."

CHAPTER 23

"These belonged to James?" Barbara took the first folder from the old chest and crinkled her nose. The bright sunlight of a new day illuminated the documents in the woven reed and brass chest, and a musty odor emanated from it. Not of mold but of crumbling acrylic and tarnished metal.

"Yes." Christy poured herself another cup of tea and sat back in the wicker chair. "After you told us about Doris's pregnancy, I thought you'd want to have them."

Agatha squared her shoulders. "Did Doris and James really have a baby, Barb?"

"Well." Barbara folded her hands in her lap. "Doris does write of being pregnant, of going to the doctor and getting the news. She was in absolute turmoil, worried out of her skull. Like I said, my grandparents had very high expectations for their daughters. My mother delivered in spades, so I imagine there was even more pressure on Doris."

"A baby out of wedlock would have been a big dark secret then." Agatha shook her head.

"Yes, very much so. She was terrified, poor thing. To the point that after she found out, Doris stopped spilling her soul onto paper, in case someone found the letters. Or...maybe something happened that convinced her he had died, I don't know. Either way, we don't know what happened with the pregnancy. But Doris wouldn't have had access to abortion doctors. And even more troubling—there is no report of a baby." Barbara glanced at her friends. "I have no cousins."

"Maybe a miscarriage? Let's see if we can find any clues in James's papers." Agatha pulled red reading glasses from the pocket of the knitted cardigan she was wearing despite the warm temperatures in the winter garden. "What's in that folder there?" She picked one from the chest.

Lukas appeared at Barbara's side, handing her her own reading glasses. Christy, too, pulled a pair off her head and onto her nose and dug up a large journal hiding behind folders and legal-sized documents.

"This looks relevant," Christy noted as she was flipping through the journal's pages. "Let's see." She cleared her throat and read.

I found the house she lived in, and I managed to talk her father into selling it to me. He didn't recognize me, nor did he remember my name. That's how much the war has changed me. It's a good thing; otherwise I doubt he'd let me buy his daughter's last abode. So now I sit and look at the ocean and miss her. My heart aches for her. Not in an abstract way, but quite literally.

The shell seeker told me where the rip tide pulled Doris under. I can't stop staring at that spot. There's no reason for it, other than a dream I had that she emerges again from the water, flipping back her wet hair, laughing at me. But she won't. Because I was in hospital, relearning how to walk, how to speak, how to eat, how to remember, instead of saving her.

Agatha raised her eyebrows. "Poor man. Poor Doris."

"It explains why we remember him sitting on the beach, watching the water," Barbara noted quietly. "That probably wasn't healthy."

"He had a broken heart," Agatha said. "And a broken heart is not a healthy thing."

Christy flipped some pages, scanning through them. "Oh, girls, here. Listen."

I bought lumber for a shed at the local mill today. The cashier is an aid to the local midwife, and when she heard I had bought the cottage, she accidentally shared a secret with me. Her words unraveled the last of my sanity. Doris had a baby, a beautiful little girl, just about nine months after I left the cove.

"He knew?" Barbara felt excitement surge through her, and it was all she could do not to rip the journal from her friend. "Does he say what happened to the baby? Is there more?"

"Not for this date. But hang on." Christy again turned some pages and took a deep breath to read.

I've caught glimpses of her from a distance—laughter like wind chimes, curls that dance in the ocean breeze. The whispers say she's mine, and my arms know it's true. They ache to hold my daughter.

I managed to meet Doris's sister, Ella. Unlike her father, she remembers me very well. She'll never forgive me for leaving Doris when she needed me most. She was so angry with me she could barely look me in the eye.

Christy looked up. "Then there are a couple of empty pages," she said quietly.

"Read what's next." Barbara was looking at her hands, which were trembling slightly.

"Let me see if there's more." Christy skipped through pages, muttering as she scanned the entries.

"Lukas, do you mind making more tea?" Agatha handed the butler the empty tea pot.

He inclined his head in a stiff bow and disappeared. When he returned, he brought Margrit and a tray of cookies.

Christy cleared her throat. "Here goes. I skipped over some pondering of life and thoughts on his art. He must've been pretty lonely." She read.

She came to the cottage today to talk to me, on the condition that I stop writing her letters. I understand her better now. Ella risked everything to keep Doris from becoming destitute. Ella's husband left a week after me for a year-long diplomatic mission abroad. With only two doting servants in the house, the sisters swapped their roles of mother and aunt.

Barbara's nails dug into her palms in shock, and her sudden intake of breath made everyone look up. "Read," she rasped, her throat dry as old driftwood. "Read it all." Her eyes as wide as the fine china saucers on the table, Christy obliged.

Ella insisted that I respect her wishes regarding the child, and though it pained me, I agreed. It's clear that Ella and her husband dote on Barbara. In my weakened state after the war, I know that claiming her would only bring turmoil to her life. I can see that she is content and cared for—Barbara is a picture of happiness, always cared for by adoring nannies and Ella, who is never far away.

I may not be able to offer the luxuries that Barbara enjoys in Ella's care, but I find solace in knowing that she is cherished and protected. My only wish is to be close by in case she ever needs me, ready to offer whatever support and love I can provide. It may not be much, but it's the least I can do for my daughter and her mother. It brings me some small measure of peace.

"Oh, the poor man. What a terrible thing war is, ripping families apart like that." Margrit put a hand on Barbara's shoulder and squeezed. "Dear me, Barb."

"But..." Barbara blinked. "*Ella* is my mother," she protested, feeling numb.

"Maybe James is only spinning yarn." Agatha leaned forward. "But honestly, he sounds pretty sincere. It's possible that Ella is your aunt," she said gently. "If James is telling the truth, you are the missing baby yourself, Barb."

"It doesn't change anything," Lukas said, his deep voice reassuring. "You're your mother's daughter. She raised you, and she loved you. So did your father."

For a brief moment, Barbara put her hand on Margrit's that still rested on her shoulder. Then she took a deep breath, trying to shake off her shock. "Lukas, Margrit, do you two think you could get lunch ready?"

"I like them a lot," Agatha said, wistfully looking after the pair as they left. "I wish I had servants."

"I don't use that word." Barbara squared her shoulders. "They're more like employees."

"They're more like friends who happen to work in this house," Christy noted, peering over the brim of her reading glasses. "I'm glad you all have each other."

"I went to James's funeral," Barbara said suddenly. "It was only my mother and me and a few of our staff there. Everyone threw a flower and a handful of soil onto the coffin. But Mother told me to toss three handfuls, not one. It's an old tradition, I found out later, reserved for only the family of the deceased." She sighed and took off her reading glasses, pinching her nose. "I cried. I was so sad for the old man. He always seemed so lonely."

"If this turns out to be true—would you have wanted to know?" Christy asked.

Barbara sank back into the cushions of her sofa, glancing up at the gracefully arched ceiling. "How can I decide something like that? I loved my parents very much." She hesitated. "But my little toddler heart loved Doris too. I would have liked to know her better. I would have liked to talk with James while he was still around." She frowned, suddenly feeling frustrated. "I would have liked to *know*! I wish they'd told me! Maybe James couldn't make my life better. But it's quite possible that I could have improved his life."

"It's possible your dad, lovely as I'm sure he was, would've had a problem with that." Christy poured them all fresh tea. "Who knows? Maybe James and Ella did the right thing, keeping it a secret." She sat back and sighed. "Do you want to do a DNA test?"

"With what, my father's ashes?" Barbara lifted her cup to drink, trying to calm herself. "Honestly, I'm confused about what I think and what I want. The only thing I do know is that no matter what, I would like to go to the cemetery and bring Doris and James roses." She lowered her tea again. "You know, they were buried in the same cemetery."

"Then we'll do that," Agatha said gently. "And we can do it right now."

Barbara looked at the cup she was holding in midair. It trembled lightly, the tea sloshing from side to side, dangerously close to the brim. "Hold on, Agatha," she said, noticing a light tremble in her voice as well. "I do believe I'll have a cup of tea first."

CHAPTER 24

The breeze rustled like a melancholy soul in the ancient cypress trees, and the gray sky draped like a blanket over the gate of the foggy cemetery.

"Of course the weather has to be like that." Barbara glanced at the leaden clouds above while Lukas closed the car doors. "My hat is going to fly away."

"Then take it off," Agatha recommended. "It's windy, not cold. It doesn't matter if you wear a hat or not."

Christy tightened the silk scarf she wore over her silver curls. "Agatha's right. Just leave the hat in the car."

"Oh, all right." Shifting the bouquet of velvety red roses into her other hand, Barbara handed her black hat to Lukas, who sighed and stowed it away. "I thought I'd at least dress properly," she grumbled.

"What counts is that you're here to pay your respects." Christy hooked one arm under Barbara's and the other under Agatha's.

"Do you want me to come, or should I wait?" Lukas ran a hand through his windblown hair, trying to get it out of his eyes.

"Come with me, please," Barbara said, looking over her shoulder. "If you don't mind."

He smiled and nodded. It was the encouragement Barbara had needed.

She exhaled, trying to relax. "I know exactly where Doris's headstone is. And I think James's isn't far off, but I'll need a look." Lukas bringing up the rear, they started walking, awkwardly at first because their arms were linked to each other. But soon, they found their rhythm.

When they reached the row where her family rested, Barbara let go of her friends. "Doris is next to my mother—or rather, my aunt," she said quietly.

"Which one is it?" Agatha asked, clutching her knitted blue coat tight against the wind. She leaned in, squinting at the names engraved in the granite stone markers. "These are all Bakers."

"My mother's the tall stone angel over there. And when I say my mother, I mean Ella. Oh, this will never not feel strange." Barbara exhaled, walking faster. In a way, she'd come to terms with the fact that Doris's letters and James's diary likely told the truth. But in another way, she was still in disbelief.

The confusion over her lineage had barely settled over the past week. Questions bubbled under the surface of her calm demeanor, and a few times she'd feared it was too much and that she would boil over in a sudden, unsolvable, uncleanable mess.

"I'm going to stick to calling the people who raised me my mother and father."

Christy stopped to untie her fluttering silk scarf, muttering, "This thing never stays on."

"Ma'am? Here—I'll keep it safe for you." Lukas reached out and took the scarf, folding it neatly and putting it into the pocket of his jacket.

"Oh!" Christy smiled at him. "Thank you very much."

"Can we all have a Lukas?" Agatha murmured. "Aha! There's your mother, Ella."

Barbara joined her in front of her mother's grave. "And this is Dad beside her." She separated five roses for each parent and laid them on the marble plaques. "I love you both," she whispered. "Whatever it is you did." She cleared her throat and took a few steps to the side, coming to stand before the smaller headstone to the left of the angel.

"Doris Meinhardt—beloved sister, taken too soon," she read the engraving. "My mother insisted on being close to her too."

"They stuck together," Christy murmured. "I wish I'd have been half the sister Ella was."

"My mother truly risked everything by pretending I was her baby," Barbara said. "Dad *can't* have known." She chewed on her lip, half-buried feelings slowly forming into thoughts. "Or maybe..."

"What do you mean, maybe?" Christy glanced over.

"Well...between us girls and Lukas, I'm not sure my dear father was always loyal to my mother."

"How do you know?" Christy whispered and glanced over her shoulder as if they were speaking of state secrets.

Barbara shrugged, a little embarrassed. "There were an awful lot of money gifts given to women in his will.

I've come to peace with the fact that he lived his life as he saw fit. But while I'm certain Ella was always faithful to him—it turns out that in the end, the child she gave him might not have been his after all."

"Give a little, take a little," Agatha murmured.

Barbara smiled. "Something like that. I have to say...the more I think about it, the more it makes sense."

"Like what?" Christy glanced at her.

"When Doris found out she was pregnant, my mother saw the opportunity that my father's absence gave them." Barbara wiped her hair back. "Doris moved into the house, supposedly to care for Ella. Really, they were hiding that it was Doris who was pregnant, aided and abetted by Ella's doting staff. Once I was born, it was easy. Ella had a baby, and Doris moved back into the cottage. The only witness was the staff, a midwife, and one chatty aide."

"Giving you up can't have been easy for Doris." Christy frowned.

"Maybe by giving me to Ella, she did keep me." Barbara shook her head. "My grandparents might not have allowed Doris to keep me. I might have been sent to some cruel place for illegitimate children."

"Oh dear," Agatha whispered. "Then it kind of worked out for the best, didn't it?"

"If my happiness was the sisters' goal, then yes. I was happy." Slowly, Barbara set ten roses from her garden on Doris's grave, letting her fingers trail over the pitted stone. "I'm sorry I never got to know you better," she whispered. "But I miss you anyway. Whatever you did for me—thank you."

She swallowed as tears started to press up her throat. Why couldn't Doris and Ella have had each other's back without having to hide? Why was it so hard for women and—

"Ma'am?" Lukas, who'd been wandering about, put a warm hand on her arm. "I believe it's starting to rain."

"Really?" Barbara let him help her up, wiping her cheek. There was no point asking why and when. It was a different time, with different rules, and different people. "Where's James's grave?" She rubbed her forehead, trying to remember.

"Right on the other side of the cypress here. Take my arm."

Barbara leaned on his arm as they walked over. Not because her muscles were weak but because it made her feel safe when everything around her was swirling, rearranging itself in new patterns.

"James rests next to Doris," Agatha noted. "There's only that big old tree between them. Is that by accident?"

"No," Lukas said quietly. "Mrs. Baker ordered it. My father worked for her, and I remember him telling me about it."

Barbara glanced at him. Lukas's parents had both worked for her parents. "You wouldn't know anything more about Doris, would you?"

"I would have told you already," he replied. "Doris was as much before my time as it was before yours."

"Yes." She leaned closer to him, breathing in his familiar, calming scent of fresh newspapers and aromatic tea. "Yes, of course."

"Would you like me to come back and clean up James's headstone?" he asked.

"Thank you, but no." Barbara let go of him to put down the last of her roses. "I will come back and do it myself. Well, maybe we can come together. You can help me. If you want, I mean."

"Of course I do," Lukas said. "I'll always be there for you."

CHAPTER 25

Christy tilted the patio umbrella to shade the tasty offerings on her new patio table. She didn't want them to dry out in the sun because this was a premiere. A few weeks after moving into her cottage, she had finally baked something in her kitchen. The inspiration had been a couple of her mother's recipes that had fallen out of an old book Christy was reading. Ready for the challenge, she'd shoved up her sleeves and gone to work.

Streaks of batter and smears of butter had covered every inch of everything by the time she was pushing the form into the oven, and she'd had to call Agatha with a question every minute or so. But it had worked out. One of the attempts had manifested into a real, moist, rich madeira cake. Infused with honey and thyme, the fragrance unearthed a long-lost memory of baking with her mother in the kitchen. Touched, Christy lit a candle for her mom.

The other baking success was a sheet full of apricot and almond tartlets. They looked a little wonky but smelled of marzipan and glistened temptingly.

"Hello there!" Ethan came walking around the side of the house, waving a bouquet at her. "You look lovely, Christy." He came to kiss her on her cheeks. "Not that you need more, surrounded by flowers as you are," he murmured in her ear, "but these are for you."

"Thank you." Christy took the bouquet into her arms. Arranging flower bouquets had, to her surprise, quickly become a new hobby. "And this is for you." She stood on her tiptoes and kissed him on the mouth. He tried to kiss her back, but smiling, she sank back on her heels.

It had been a month ago that he brought over the gramophone. The evening could have led to more, but he'd respected her wishes and slowed down. They ate and drank wine and danced to the LPs from the flea market, but then he'd left and gone home.

"Mmm." He exhaled and ran a hand through his hair. "Is this still the friend zone then?"

"You were *never* in my friend zone, Ethan." She lifted her eyebrows.

"I guess not, since you just kissed me." His arms went around her, pulling her closer. "Does that mean I can kiss you too whenever I want? Or are we doing this only one-way?"

"Should we do it only one-way?" His arm tightened again, and Christy stifled a giggle.

"That'd be extremely unfair, but what can I say? I played all my cards when I told you that I'll take whatever it is you give me." He lowered his head, his lips hovering over hers. "Better answer me quickly, though, gorgeous."

"I'm in my *sixties*," she protested, still laughing.

"Doesn't make a difference to me. You'll always be my Barb." He closed the last of the gap between them, pressing his lips to hers and kissing her fully for the first time since the vineyard.

"Mmm." She put her hands on his chest and pushed gently. "Hey."

"What?" He released his hold, his eyes searching hers.

"I baked, Ethan. I baked us a cake."

His eyes softened, and he smiled. "You baked us a cake? Is it edible?"

"Yes. At least, I think so. The batter was yummy." She took his hand. Her heart was hammering like it had when she'd been twenty, but it felt good. The weeks of dating had settled any feeling that this was a repeat of the past. They took the time to get to know each other again. They talked more about Abby, about life and themselves, telling of their struggles and triumphs, their flings and relationships, their hopes and dreams for the future.

When the sunshine had woken Christy this morning, she knew she no longer needed to test the waters. Ethan was here. He wanted her, she wanted him, and they belonged together. Suddenly, everything felt crystal clear.

"Well, whatever you made, I'll try it." He sat in the chair she pulled out for him.

She sat on the other chair and poured them both coffee. "Ethan?"

"Yes?"

"I have news for you." She smiled. "It's about the painting you found at the flea market."

He blinked, and then he chuckled. "I forgot about that. Did you have a look at it?"

"Yes. I did. I had a very, *very* careful look at it. In fact, I drove all the way to San Francisco to look."

Ethan's eyebrows rose, and he leaned back, crossing his arms expectantly. "Really. Why?"

"Because I needed some equipment I don't have here." Christy looked at her hands on the table, still seeing them shake those of old colleagues and peer experts. Then she looked back up. "I was glad to find that some of my former colleagues are still ready to help me out."

A smile of satisfaction spread across his face. "Then the dust has settled?"

"They didn't seem ashamed to know me."

"Of course not. I knew they'd come around." He shook his head. "They can't let go of you that easily. Nobody can."

"Thank you." She smiled back at him. "Anyway, you'll never guess who painted your aquarelle."

"Who?"

Christy named the contemporary artist as well as the price the painting would likely fetch at auction. "He's highly collectible right now," she confided. "If you're thinking about selling, there'll never be a better moment."

"You aren't serious." He straightened his back. "That's a lot—a *lot*—of money."

"I am serious. I'm sure it's an early Costa. Of course you could hang it in your house. I'm just letting you know what you found there."

"And you are *sure?*"

She laughed. "I'm sure."

"Then authenticate the painting."

"Oh. No—there's a Costa foundation for that. They're the ones who will do it."

He smiled. "Are you saying that because you aren't sure after all?"

"I'm one hundred percent sure. I just happen to not belong to the Costa foundation." She tapped a finger against her lips. "Are you trying to give me my confidence back?"

He opened his hands, defenseless. "Can you blame me? You're fantastic."

"Well." Shaking her head, Christy reached for the coffee carafe and refilled their cups. "It does feel good. It does remind me that I know my stuff—and that I enjoy this work."

"I'll send it to the foundation," Ethan promised. "And once *they'll* authenticate it, I want you to bring it to auction. If that doesn't show them, nothing will."

Christy set the carafe down and narrowed her eyes. "Show who what, exactly?"

"Show your auction house what they lost when they let you leave. They'll be falling over themselves to get you back now."

"If I *want* to be back," she said mildly, but then she threw up her hands. "Who am I kidding? I do want that. I still love art. I still want to be part of that world, at least a little bit."

She let her gaze wander over the glistening blue Pacific that stretched to the horizon, the garden that Billie and Agatha and she had cut from the weeds, the cute little pottery studio she'd set up in Jim's old shed. "This is where I want to live. But I enjoyed visiting the city and talking about artists and taking a few X-rays to unravel the mystery. Yes, I still would like all that to play a part in my life."

"I know," he replied. "I'm retired too. But I have a lot of skills that I enjoy putting to good use."

"Exactly." She pressed her lips together. "Ethan, tell me the truth."

"About what?"

"Did you really find the Costa at the flea market? Or has it been hanging on a wall in your house for years already?"

"Erm." He ran a hand through his hair, but then he dropped it. "I'm caught fair and square, and I knew it would happen eventually. To be honest, it was hanging in my house for a while."

"Hmm." She took a tartlet and bit into it. It was delicious—filled with almond frangipane Agatha had talked her through making and topped with glazed apricots for both nuttiness and fruity sweetness. "I don't like that you lied to me."

"I *didn't* lie—only a teensy bit by omission. I did find it under a stack of comics at a flea market like I told you, just not the flea market where we met. I thought it could be a Costa, but not being an expert, I was never sure," he said. "Please forgive me. I was just trying to take away the pressure. I wanted to help you get back in the game. And it worked, didn't it?"

"It worked," she admitted and leaned toward him. "But don't do it again."

He shook his head. "I'll lie and cheat and steal to make you smile, my dear. That's just how it's going to be.""No, none of that." Christy, chuckling against her will, waved his protest away. "Tell me—the flea market took place in '89, in San Diego. Correct?"

His eyes widened. "1990! How did you know?"

"I traced the painting all the way to that city and that time. It *must* be the lost piece." Triumphantly, Christy fell back in her chair. "Authenticating it would mean we'll be officially editing the Catalogue Raisonné. That would be...big. Huge."

"I'm glad." He smiled tentatively. "So am I forgiven?"

"At least you didn't lie again when I asked you," she decided. "And I was already set on giving you a second chance when I woke up this morning."

"You're giving me a second chance?" He leaned forward, catching her meaning immediately.

"Yes." She looked at him. "If you still want it."

"I do, Christy." Ethan reached for her hand on the table, taking it into his own. "Thank you for this, for giving us another chance. There's nowhere I'd rather be than here, with you."

Their fingers intertwined, and silence settled between them. Not awkward but filled with the unspoken promises of a shared future. Even the garden seemed to hold its breath.

Then Ethan stood, offering his hand to Christy, who also rose to her feet. "I don't want to eat when I can hold your hand instead. Shall we take a stroll by the sea?" Gently, he pulled her into his arms.

Smiling, she looked up at him. They were so close she had to tilt her head into her neck. "Is this what you call holding hands?" she whispered.

Instead of answering, he lowered his head and kissed her again. Unlike their quick kiss before, this one was deep as the ocean, rich like old wine, and full of questions to which Christy finally knew the answer.

She pulled away to trail a finger from his ear to his chin, tracing the familiar outline of his jaw, feeling the cleanly shaved skin. "You know that new window you built upstairs?"

"The one in your bedroom?" His voice was low and full of gravel, a river ready to break the dam and sweep her away. "What about it?"

"Yes—well, my new bed frame was finally delivered, and I was wondering whether you'd like to come upstairs and admire how well it fits under your window."

He pulled her back to him, encircling her waist, pressing her to his chest, making her laugh. "Are you asking me whether I want to check out your bed?" His lips moved against her neck, sending shivers of desire down her body.

"That's not what I...but yes." Again she laughed. "Yes, Ethan, that's exactly what I'm asking." It didn't matter anymore that she was suddenly sixty and that they both had silver in their hair. The only thing that mattered was they loved each other, had always loved each other. Despite mistakes and misgivings and misunderstandings and all the other things that so easily divert the course of youth, inexperience, and hearts that don't yet know themselves.

"I thought you'd never ask!" With a growl, Ethan lifted Christy in his arms. "Making that window and thinking of you waking up there, hair mussed up and sleepy eyed and warm almost drove me crazy."

Despite her laughter and her protest, Ethan carried Christy over the threshold into the kitchen and up the stairs, just as strong and eager as she had always remembered him.

CHAPTER 26

A gatha?" The voice coming from the speaker buzzed with static.

"Yes. Who's this?" Agatha pushed her gardening hat back and wiped the sweat off her forehead. She didn't know the number. But the extended car warranty guys didn't usually call her by her first name, did they?

"It's me. Marlene. Hang on a moment, I have to..." Suddenly, the static stopped. "Is that better? I'm out of the forest."

Marlene, Bobby's wife? She and Agatha rarely talked on the phone. Usually, it was Bobby who called her. Gripping her phone tighter, Agatha let go of the rhododendron she'd been pruning. "Yes, that's better. How are you, Marlene? Is everything okay?" Frowning, she walked into the shade of the old willow and sat on one of the Adirondack chairs. "Is something wrong with Ryan?" Or the baby? Suddenly scared, Agatha gripped the arm rest.

"Ryan's fine! We're all fine. Is this a bad time?"

Agatha took a deep breath. "No, I'm out in the garden, pottering around."

"That sounds nice." Marlene's quiet laugh put Agatha more at ease than any reassurances. "Actually, Agatha, I was wondering if you were busy this afternoon. Bobby's going to pick up Ryan from school today, and I'm on my way to Mendocino Cove."

Agatha sat up straight, as much as one could in a wooden bucket seat. "You're coming here? Why?"

"I have an appointment to look at a house. And I wanted to ask if you'd like to join me."

"Join you...looking at a house?" Agatha felt her eyes widen. "Already?"

"When we left your place after the dinner, we didn't go straight back home." Again, Marlene's quiet laugh. "We meant to, but then the village looked so adorable, and we parked in front of the Mermaid Galley and got out to walk around the village a little bit. Bobby got into talking with someone fixing up their fence."

"Which house?" Agatha asked.

"It's on Almond Lane. The last one before you turn into...uh, I don't remember the name. The street with the market on it."

"That's Mary's house."

"Yes! We talked to her son."

Agatha tapped a finger on her knee, digging for the name. "That's Payton. He doesn't live in the cove but comes once a month to look after the house. Mary's arthritis is playing up. The last time we talked, she was looking into assisted living. It's not far away, and she wants to stay in town."

"Yes, exactly. Her son said they wanted to sell the house. I'm going to have a look. And I was hoping you'd have time to come with me. I'd like your opinion."

Agatha relaxed back into her chair, taking off her straw hat to fan herself. It was a hot, bright spell for this time of the year, and even in the shade of the willow, the air was sun-dappled and warm. "Sure, honey. I'd love to come."

Marlene was a great mom and a good wife to Bobby. But much as Agatha liked her daughter-in-law, they had rarely done something just the two of them. There had been the usual dinners and weekends, but those had always included other people.

Marlene didn't sound worried at all. Her voice was light and happy when she said, "Great! Well, I'm already on my way. I'm going to be there in half an hour. Does that work for you?"

"That works." Agatha hauled herself upright. "I need a quick shower. I need to...uh, sweetheart, you should get off the phone if you're driving. It's not safe."

One more time, Marlene laughed her calming laugh. "I'm using Bluetooth, Agatha. The connection is hands-free. But you're right. Fern Beach is coming up with a bunch of exits, and I always get nervous about the lane change. I'll meet you at your place, okay?"

"Yes, okay. Make sure to..." She had no idea what exit Marlene needed to take. "I don't know either." She exhaled. "But good luck! I'll see you in half an hour."

They ended the call. "They are really doing it," Agatha whispered. They had said they would, at the dinner. She'd lain awake at night, wondering if it was too early to propose available houses to them. She slapped her gardening hat back on her head and went into the house.

Twenty-five minutes later, Agatha was showered and dressed in her best blue dress, sandals on her feet. She was standing in the kitchen, wondering whether she should brew tea, when she heard a car drive up the street and hurried to the front door.

The car coming up the street was a minivan, and out of the driver's window, Marlene was waving.

"Hey!" Agatha waved back. "You're five minutes early! The lane changes worked out."

"I know!" Marlene called back from the open window. She parked and got out of the van. "I got the right exit on the first try."

Agatha smiled and pulled her daughter-in-law in for a hug. "Good for you."

Marlene hugged her back. "Are you ready? I don't want to be late and risk him leaving."

Agatha grabbed her purse and pulled her door shut behind her. "Let's go." They hopped back into the van.

Using Agatha's small driveway, Marlene turned around. "Thank you for coming with me. I really didn't want to go on my own; I want someone to talk it through afterward."

"What about Bobby? He didn't want to come?" Agatha strapped herself in. She couldn't remember the last time she'd been in an unfamiliar car. It smelled of melted candy bars and Ryan's soccer gear, and there was an empty water bottle rattling under her seat. She smiled and picked it up, stowing it in her door to throw away later.

"Bobby would've liked to come, but he has a big meeting today." Marlene flicked the blinker and turned. "He thinks it could be about the promotion."

"Then he should go," Agatha said. "Are you sure that's what it is?"

"Almost." Marlene smiled. "His boss is a big one for dropping hints, so cross your fingers Bobby read him right."

They drove into the village, the true center of Mendocino Cove, and Marlene parked in front of the Mermaid Galley. "I took the rest of the day off," she said as they got out. "After looking at the house, I thought we could have a cup of tea here if you still have time. Bobby's forever talking about the food at this place."

"I have time if you do," Agatha said and squinted up at the restaurant that looked out at the bluff and the ocean. A couple of familiar faces were visible behind the big windows. Billie, Ava, Faye, and Jenny, laughing and eating what looked like big bowls of raspberries and whipped cream.

Marlene joined Agatha on the small sidewalk and hooked her arm under her mother-in-law's. Her smile was infectious. "I'm so excited to see this house; I was dreaming about it last night. It looks so cute from the outside, and it has a lovely garden. I've always wanted one, though I don't know the first thing about gardening."

"It's not hard. You plant flowers, and then you water them."

Marlene chuckled. "I'm sure there's more to it than that."

"Maybe." The corners of Agatha's lips curved upward. "I could show you a trick or two."

"Yes." Marlene smiled back. "If we really do get a garden in the end, I would love that."

CHAPTER 27

H ello! You're right on time. Come on in. Oh, and
you brought a friend!" Payton opened the gate in
the wooden fence, waving Marlene and Agatha inside
the blooming garden.

"Don't you remember me?" Smiling, Agatha closed
the gate behind her. Mary used to have a fat tabby cat.
Mary wouldn't like for him to get out.

Payton pushed his baseball cap back and then held
out his hand. "Agatha! Yes, of course I remember you.
It's been a while. How are you?"

"Fine." She shook his hand. "How is your mother?"

"She's good." He nodded in confirmation of his
words. "She's taking a trip to the Grand Canyon with
a couple of friends before moving into the senior residence. She said that if she has to set sail and move out
of this house, she'll do it in style. They've rented one
of those humongous RVs." He shook his head as if his
mother's adventure worried him.

But Agatha liked the idea. Mary had never been one
to mope around. "Is she having fun?"

"Yes, I'd have to say that she is. The friends who are
with her are moving into the same residence. They all

bought apartments next to each other." He took out a tissue from his pocket and wiped his forehead, looking resigned. "She's having a good old time."

"Good, I'm glad." Looking relieved, Marlene put a hand to her heart. "That makes me feel much better."

Payton grinned. "Yeah, don't worry about Mom having to sell. She and her friends were planning this for a long time, and she's looking forward to not having to maintain a big old creaky Victorian." He stuffed his tissue back in his pocket. "Do you want a tour to see if you'd like to take it on?"

"Yes, absolutely. I'm so ready for a creaky old Victorian; you have no idea." Marlene eagerly followed Payton inside, checking over her shoulder to make sure Agatha was coming along.

Smiling, Agatha did. She already knew the house, and she knew the space and commodities would work for the young family. It was really only a question of style; Marlene was used to modern apartments, not old houses.

"Well, this is the living room." Payton stood aside, smiling sheepishly because he had to wipe his forehead again. "It's hot today."

"That it is." Agatha immediately saw that Payton had been hard at work in the house, sprucing it up for the sale.

"It's just as pretty inside as outside!" Marlene exclaimed. "I thought it'd be furnished in a more old-fashioned style, but it's perfect!" Suddenly realizing that it wasn't the politest thing to say, she covered her mouth. "I didn't... I'm sorry!" She dropped her hand, laughing at herself. "I shouldn't have said that."

"Nah, it's okay. I know what you mean." Payton grinned and slapped his hat back on. "Mom likes to watch soap operas and always said it was a good way to keep up with the times. She's all about fashion and furniture." Satisfied at Marlene's reaction, he looked around. "I'm glad you like the style since it'd be great if you could take it off my hands together with the house. I already moved everything we want to keep, and I don't exactly want to haul the rest over the mountain range and pay to put it in storage, if you know what I mean. If you're interested, I'll give you a good price."

"I'll certainly keep that in mind." Payton moved on to the dining room, and Marlene turned to make big, longing eyes at Agatha, who nodded back.

Whatever soaps Mary had been watching must have been set in seaside houses, because the wide, light couches, cheerful, multicolored pillows, the earth-colored Sisal rugs and runners were beautiful. So was the sprinkling of wooden tables and bookshelves, pretty lamps, and plants in gorgeous pots that deepened and brightened the space.

Agatha went to the open window and pushed the white, gauzy curtains back. "Marlene, come look at this."

Her daughter-in-law came and looked out the window. "I can see the sea from here! I had no idea!"

"You can see the sea from the kitchen too!" Payton called out.

Marlene and Agatha dropped the curtains, leaving the breeze to play with them, and went through an elegant yet cozy dining room with tall, built-in hatches into the kitchen.

"Stove, fridge, double sink." Payton pointed at the wide window over the sink. "You can see the ferry go between the cove and the island while you do the dishes." Busily, he turned around. "Mom wants the kitchen table in her new apartment, but there's another table in the garden shed that's brand-new. What do you think?"

"I think it's beautiful." Marlene leaned over the spotless white porcelain sink to touch one of the flowering orchids on the windowsill. "How pretty are these?"

"A few of them are still destined for Mom's new apartment too," Payton admitted. "But you can get them at the florist in Pebble Beach. And Mom can tell you all about how to get them to flower every year."

Marlene's smile at the thought of caring for her orchid collection brightened the room. "It sounds nice."

Payton nodded. "I don't mean to put pressure on you, but I have to tell you—this house won't last long once I put it on the market. I'm only showing it to you before listing because Bobby is Agatha's son. Mom would like it if local friends took the house. She's already chewed me out five times over for not moving in myself, but there's no way. My wife is happy where we are, and I'm not about to open a can of worms."

"No." Agatha patted his arm. "Don't do that."

"I really appreciate that you're doing this," Marlene said. "Thank you, Payton. Your mom too. Wherever we go from here—please let her know I adore the house."

The heartfelt tone of the words brought a smile to Agatha's face. If Bobby truly did get that promotion... Marlene was clearly already in love with the house. What if it all worked out? What if she'd have her family move back to Mendocino Cove? With anticipation coursing through her veins, Agatha drew in a deep, exhilarated breath.

"Are you okay? Do you want to sit down?" Marlene turned to her. "I'll just have a quick look upstairs."

"I'm fine. I'm fine. But you're right—I'll sit in the garden. I know the upstairs; I've been up there before. Have a look, and then come find me to tell me how you like it."

"If you want lemonade, there's plenty in the fridge." Payton opened a cabinet and put glasses on the counter. "There's snacks as well. Help yourself."

"Thank you. Take your time. I'll be happy as a clam outside." Agatha waited until the two disappeared, first stopping by the laundry room. Quiet murmurs about washers and dryers drifted across the corridor, and then Marlene laughed.

Satisfied, Agatha went to pour herself a glass of lemonade. She'd have to stop by Mary's new apartment once Mary was settled. Maybe Agatha and Christy and Barbara, once their time came, would also move together? The old mansion was certainly big enough for them all.

Agatha went back out into the warm sun and found the bench that was hidden among the honeysuckle and wisteria. She sat, more excited and hopeful for the future than she'd been in years. If only Bobby was right about the promotion, the puzzle pieces would fall perfectly into place. She leaned back into the honeysuckle, willing it to be so and forbidding herself to consider any other options. Bobby's boss simply had to deliver the good news.

CHAPTER 28

Agatha sipped her lemonade, letting the sun counteract the ice in it, and decided to count butterflies to keep calm, the way one counts sheep during the night.

A handful of monarchs dipped in search of milkweed, their gorgeous orange-and-black wings calling for attention. A peacock butterfly fluttered over her head and landed on a purple cluster of blooming wisteria. By the time Agatha heard the kids clatter back down the stairs, she had also spotted a swallowtail, a red admiral, and two painted ladies visiting the roses. Tiny bees in shimmering greens and blues also looked for nectar, and fat, fuzzy bumble bees hummed busily from sweet-smelling flower to sweet-smelling flower, their thick furs dusted yellow and white with pollen.

"Over here!" Agatha shaded her eyes and squinted up at the young people when they came outside to join her. Marlene came to her, her face filled with bubbly excitement, cheeks flushed with happiness.

"So I guess that's the house," Payton said and picked up his rake from the fence to lean on the wooden handle. "Can I answer any questions?"

"I already chewed your ears off." Marlene smiled. "And I'm starving. Can I get back to you by tomorrow? When will you list the house?"

"Next week at the earliest," Payton replied comfortably. "If I don't hear from you, I'll check in before the house hits the market."

"It won't be long," Marlene promised. "I just have to check in with the husband."

He nodded and shooed a honeybee away. "You do that."

Agatha and Marlene thanked Payton for the tour and the lemonade, and then they left.

"Oh. My. Goodness," Marlene whispered when they were out of earshot. "Agatha, it's so beautiful! I'm dying!"

"You are?" Agatha felt a huge smile spread over her face. "You are? Are you really?"

"Yes! Yes, really, really, really. I'm so in love, I was scared I'd burst out screaming!"

Agatha pulled open the door to the restaurant and looked at her daughter-in-law. Her eyes were shining, and her cheeks were so flushed that Agatha had to laugh with joy and relief. "You were so quiet; I was starting to think it was too cottage-core for you after all!"

"No, I love everything about that house! I'd call Bobby right now, only I'm afraid my hands are trembling." Marlene laughed. Not her usual, quiet laugh, but a loud laughter, high and bright, like that of a child. "I can't believe the timing! I can't believe... I can't believe we're this lucky!"

"Good." Agatha let the door fall shut behind them and led the way upstairs so they would have a view while they ate. She didn't want to ruin Marlene's parade, but the deal wasn't done yet. "But listen, darling...do you know whether Bobby got the promotion yet?"

Marlene swallowed, putting a hand on her stomach. "No. You're right. I have to be... He said he'd call me as soon as he was done with the meeting."

"Are you okay?" Agatha let her gaze drop to the hand rubbing the pregnant belly. "There I am, sitting in the garden with my iced lemonade, while you're the one pregnant and running around. Here. Sit." She pulled out a chair for Marlene.

"Yes. Thank you. I'm...oh, goodness." Marlene's eyes widened, and her other hand flew to her belly. "Agatha!" Her fingers spread over her belly. "I swear, I just felt movement!"

"She moved?" Agatha blinked.

"There! There it is again!" Marlene took Agatha's hand and pressed it onto her white shirt.

Agatha felt two soft, sweet taps on her palm. "I can feel her!" She waited, but the baby did not tap again. Agatha exhaled and straightened. "That was her, wasn't it? I just felt Lindsey!"

"There were little flutters before." Marlene pressed her own hands back on her belly, her face reflecting Agatha's excitement. "But never like this! Never so much that I could feel it with my hands."

"Maybe *you* should call Bobby." Agatha sank on her own chair, opposite her daughter-in-law. "You have to tell him."

"Hey, you two." Hannah had appeared, looking from one woman to the other, notepad at the ready. She raised an eyebrow and nodded at Marlene. "What's going on here? Is that a baby bump I see?"

"My baby just kicked for the first time." Marlene leaned back, blinking happily.

"Congrats." Hannah nodded knowingly. "That's awesome."

Something in her voice made Agatha tip her head. "Hannah? Don't tell me you're pregnant too?"

"Oh wow. Wow." Hannah grinned and tossed her dreadlocks. "Uh. No?"

"You are?" In a state of disbelief, Agatha's eyes widened. "You *are* pregnant! I can see it!"

"Hush, Agatha!" Hannah chuckled and looked over her shoulder. Then she straightened and with both hands, flattened her oversized blue T-shirt over her stomach. It stuck out in a round little ball. "Almost five months. It's a secret, all right? I don't need everyone trying to touch my belly when I serve them their clam chowder."

"Five months? Me too! Well, almost. We'll be having our babies at the same time!" Marlene's thrilled whisper carried through the room.

Hannah laughed. "Hush! That's fabulous. You don't live here, do you? I'd love to have some babies for playdates."

Marlene's chair creaked softly as she leaned back, her eyes alight with excitement. "I'm moving here. Whether my husband is coming or not."

Agatha blinked rapidly. "Of course he's coming. Right?"

Marlene laughed. "I hope so. But I can't wait any longer. I have to call him right now."

"I'm going to bring you two iced peach tea," Hannah decided. "And lobster and fries. Whatever you had going on today, you look like you're ready to celebrate."

"I want an omelet," Marlene said suddenly. "With gouda cheese."

Hannah laughed. "Sure, Mama, you got it. Whatever sounds good."

"Wait!" Agatha held out a hand as if she wanted to grab Hannah. "Wait."

"What?" Pushing her pen behind her ear, Hannah looked back over her shoulder.

Agatha lowered her voice. "It's Michael's, isn't it?"

Hannah grinned. "None of your business, ma'am." She winked, and then she sashayed off to find them iced tea and lobster tails and gouda cheese.

"It'd *better* be Michael's," Agatha muttered, casting a significant glance across the table.

"Another baby of the same age?" Smiling, Marlene opened her purse to rummage for her cell phone. "The universe is practically begging us to move here."

"By the way, how much is the house?" Agatha asked casually. The deal wasn't done yet. It was wonderful that Marlene was so excited, but not all the puzzle pieces had been put on the table yet.

Marlene put the phone on the table and hung her purse back on the chair. "We'll be fine once we sell the apartment."

"How long is that going to take?"

Marlene smiled and tapped on the phone screen. "Not long at all. There's a waitlist for the building. It's pretty nice. But not as nice as a little house by the sea, Agatha."

Agatha gave up. Nothing was going to dampen Marlene's spirits now. "Let me know if you need help with the down payment."

Marlene reached out and put her hand on Agatha's. "Bobby and I have this covered. We would ask you for help if we needed it, but we're fine."

"Okay." Agatha hoped it was true. She didn't have much money, but she'd happily give up her little nest egg to bring the kids home...

"Bobby sent me a text! Actually, he sent it thirty minutes ago." Marlene swiped the notification. "His meeting must be over. Let's see what he says."

"Fingers crossed," Agatha murmured. Her stomach plummeted. What if the meeting hadn't been about the promotion after all? What if they had to wait another six months for it? What if it never happened, and the family had to stay put where they were?

Marlene's eyes flew over the few lines. Slowly, she looked up. "He's got it," she whispered. "Agatha, he's got it, and he can start next month! He's waiting for me to call and tell him about the house."

"And here we are." Oblivious to the moment, Hannah slipped two steaming plates in front of them. Marlene had a fluffy, cheesy omelet, and sides of golden hash browns and fresh fruit salad. Agatha got a steaming lobster tail, crispy fries, creamy coleslaw, and bright lemon wedges between them.

Heart pounding, Agatha waved the fragrant steam away to see her daughter-in-law. This was real... When she spoke, her voice was higher than usual; butterflies of happiness tugged on her vocal cords with tiny little feet and beating wings that tickled in her throat. "You're moving to Mendocino Cove."

Marlene opened her mouth and closed it again, and then she laughed, joy bubbling out of her. "We are! I still have to show him the pictures of the house and get his okay. But I swear, Agatha, he's going to love it whether he likes it or not. We're moving!"

"I'll bring your iced tea and plan a play date then." Grinning, Hannah tapped on the table. "Be right back. This is by far the best table today."

"Marlene." Agatha held both her hands, reaching through lobster steam and the aroma of melted cheese for her daughter-in-law. "I'm so glad you called me. I'm so glad we did this together. Congratulations! And welcome to Mendocino Cove."

CHAPTER 29

B arbara?" Lukas leaned against the door jamb leading to the winter garden.

"Yes, Lukas?" Barbara looked up from her Country Gardens magazine. Both the inside and outside doors were open to let the breeze blow through, and it was pleasantly cool in the shade of the large potted plants.

"Do you have a moment, my dear?"

She closed the magazine and studied her butler. "What are you holding in your hands?"

He pushed off the door and came to where she sat in one of the white wicker chairs. "It's a present for you." He put a large manila envelope on the pedestal table beside her.

"A present? What's this?" She picked it up and looked around searchingly. "Shoot, I don't have my glasses."

"Here." Lukas pulled a pair from his pocket and handed them to her. "Use mine."

Smiling, she took the black horn-rimmed glasses. She'd seen them on his nose a hundred times, but this was the first time he'd offered them to her. "Thank you. Sit down, you're making me nervous." She put them on.

Margrit appeared in the door, drying her hands on a kitchen towel with a pattern of green leaves and vines. "Barb?"

"Yes?" She glanced over the rim of her glasses. "What can I do for you?"

"I baked madeleines; they're still warm. Would you like some?"

"Yes, please." Barbara smiled at her cook. "If you don't mind."

Margrit nodded and looked at Lukas. "How about you, Luke?"

"Yes, thank you, Margrit."

Barbara glanced at her butler. "How about a cup of tea while you're at it?"

He tilted his head. "If you don't mind."

"How about you, Margrit? Can you join us?"

Margrit smiled a secret little smile and shook her head. "I have a visitor in the kitchen."

"Oh! Who is your visitor?" Barbara wanted to know.

Margrit leaned into the room and whispered in a whisper that carried through the thicket of potted palms and ferns, "His name is Miles. He's a jazz musician, a professor at Lizzie May University. He's *very* good."

Barbara's smile deepened. "Then don't let him leave without tasting your madeleines, Margrit."

"He helped me bake them." Margrit winked. "And he just told me that he *loves* them. *Loves* me, in italics. He looked straight into my eyes when he said it."

A smile tugged on the corner of Lukas's lips. "I'll go get the tray, Margrit. I want a quick lock; make sure he's good enough for you."

"He's a duck. Don't be mean to him." Margrit waved Lukas to come, and the two disappeared.

Barbara picked up the envelope Lukas had left on the table and pulled out a paper. It wasn't anything special, but on the top was what looked like an official seal. Studying it through his reading glasses, she read the few words on it.

"Here you are." Lukas was back. He set a silver tray of delicate sponge cakes, their outsides buttery golden and slightly crispy, on the little table.

She looked over the rim. "What's the jazz musician like?"

He nodded calmly. "Passes muster for a first impression."

"Sit, please." Barbara slid his glasses off her nose and carefully folded them up.

Lukas sat. He filled his teacup. "What do you think?"

"You bought the old schoolhouse in Mendocino Cove." She held up the deed in question. "Why are you giving me this?"

"I told you; it's a present." He lifted an eyebrow. "My mother used to be a teacher at the school, so when the town decided to sell it two years ago, I bought it and restored it. It's in working order." Lukas shifted his position, angling his body so that he could lock eyes with her. "You've been talking about a community center for Mendocino Cove, and the old school fulfills all legal requirements and zoning regulations. This could be your community center. If you want it, of course. If not, I understand." A smile crinkled his eyes. "I might still do it, though. The building is up to code, and I have all the permits."

"I don't know what to say." It was more than two years since Barbara had walked past the old building. It was tucked in a grove of ancient cypresses, and the walls had been overgrown with untamed clematis and trumpet flowers. She'd stopped to listen to a tour guide talking about the school's history, and a tourist had said how romantic the abandoned building looked.

"Tell me the truth, Lukas." She put a hand on the document. "Was this expensive? The building itself, but also the renovations you must have done, the permits, the taxes and inspections?"

The smile returned to his eyes. "That's not a polite question."

"But was it expensive?" She tilted her head.

"I do have a past as a stockbroker, you know." His smile reached his lips. "Now be nice and stop asking."

She shook her head, amused. "Why do you stay here?"

"Solely for Margrit's cooking." He nodded at the paper, his fingers lightly drumming the table between them. "So, what do you say about starting a community center in the cove? You really don't have to take it on. But I thought you'd like the idea."

She inhaled, excitement starting to prickle in her chest. There were so many people in the cove who would benefit from a place to gather. Preschool classes, art and pottery, readings, all sorts of things to bring neighbors and friends and newcomers together. "It's perfect, Luke."

He smiled. "I know, Barbie. Take it and run with it. I'm sure you'll do a ton of good. The cove needs it."

"I will. *We* will. Thank you, Lukas." Barbara reached out, putting her hand on his. His skin was warm, and touching him felt like—she let go of him and coughed lightly, clearing her throat as a momentary distraction from the flood of emotions washing over her. "I already know who I'm going to ask to lead a children's play group."

"Agatha?" He looked at his hand on the table.

"She loves children. I'm sure she'll at least get us started. And once we have enough kids, we'll hire teachers. The young people in town need jobs so they can stay. I want to hire artists and potters and writers and teachers."

Lukas's smile vanished. Not quickly, not sadly, but slowly. Like the Mendocino morning fogs that left so gently you didn't know they were gone until suddenly the sun burned and the sky was as clear as a sapphire. "Maybe your next butler will give you an abandoned library."

Barbara laid the envelope back on the table. A rushing sound filled her ears, as if the sea was suddenly rising like a wall. "What are you... What do you mean, Luke? What next butler?" The staccato of her heartbeat matched the sound. "You are not leaving, Lukas, are you?" She pressed a hand to her throat. "Don't leave me."

He flipped the hand she'd touched. Now, he was holding hers. "I have to leave, my dear." His hazel irises were like deep ponds hiding molten gold. "You know I do."

Barbara only knew that if she went in too far, she would burn up. Already, the heat crawled up her legs, waiting to take over. All she could do was close her eyes and wait for help to arrive. "What do you mean?" she whispered. She pushed the deed to the old school building back across the table with her free hand. "I don't want this. I want you to stay. I want things to stay as they are."

"No." He lifted her hand, gently uncurled her fingers, and pressed a kiss on her open palm. "You don't want that, my dear. And neither do I."

His lips ignited another fiery, trembling current on her skin. It quivered up Barbara's arm and over her shoulder and neck, burning a trail all the way to her lips. It took her a moment before she found her voice. "Lukas. What do you mean?"

"I'm moving out," he said, rubbing his thumb over the spot on her palm he'd just kissed. "I have a house that I used to rent out. But now I'll live there."

"What about me?" The words broke from Barbara's lips before she could hold them back.

"You'll hire someone else to drive you and keep track of your reading glasses, my love." The smile returned to Lukas's lips like rain after a drought. "A young man with a family that would like to stay in the cove instead of moving away just so they can find work."

"A young man?"

Lukas put his other hand over the one he was holding as well. "And you will not drink tea with him. Nor will you offer him madeleines. Neither will he be allowed to make your breakfast."

"Oh." Barbara blinked. Her heart was beating in her throat.

"I will call you, Barbie. I'll call and ask you out. Not right away. But soon." Lukas pressed another kiss into her hand, his lips burning her despite his cool words. Then he gently let go and rose. "You can say yes or no when I ask you out. One word is all I'll need." He bowed, and then he pulled another piece of paper out of the inside pocket of his suit jacket and put it on the table. "This is my resignation, Barbie. Effective immediately." A sudden, deep sigh escaped his chest, and he raked a hand through his hair. "I can't do this any longer."

Dazed, Barbara watched Lukas walk out of the door, down the grass toward the sea, toward the path that led to the mansion's small parking lot.

"Wait." She rose and grabbed his reading glasses off the table. "Wait!" She was no spring chicken, but she was in excellent shape for her age. When she wanted, she could still run. "Lukas! Wait!"

He turned around, the rising sea breeze ruffling his hair. When he saw her running after him, he frowned and opened his arms to catch her. "What? What are you doing?" His arms closed around her, hugging her, holding her safe. His eyes were only a few inches above hers when she tilted her head back. And his lips...his lips were so close she could feel their warmth on her skin.

Barbara gasped a breath to speak. "You forgot your glasses!" She held them up in the tight space between them, slipping them into his shirt pocket.

"Thank you," he murmured. "I would have missed them." Lukas lowered his head another fraction, but then a small sound escaped from deep in his throat and he straightened his back.

Barbara blinked, holding his golden eyes. "Lukas?"

"Yes?" His voice was low, a rumble in the sea.

"I say yes. It's always been yes."

Again, the slow smile she loved so much dawned on his face. "I know," he murmured. "If I didn't know, I wouldn't leave." He lowered his head and kissed her on the forehead, then let her go.

Barbara took a step back to catch her balance. The wind tugged on her wool skirt and her silver curls, but in Lukas's face, she saw that she was just as beautiful now as she'd been in her youth.

He shook his head once, as if he couldn't believe just how beautiful she was to him. His throat moved with unspoken words before he spoke. "I'll call you, my love."

"Soon. Call soon." She pressed her hands together. She knew they had to move on; she wanted to. She was more than ready. But it would also be hard to let go of the old. She was used to having him around, always, always.

He smiled and reached out to tuck a silver curl behind her ear. "Very soon."

She leaned into his hand. "I'll be here."

Lukas drew in a breath that lifted his chest, and then he turned and walked away, his long strides turning a page and starting a new chapter.

CHAPTER 30

"Aunt Christy? Is that you?" The female voice on the
phone wavered, barely audible over the rushing
of the ocean and the trumpeting sea lion that patrolled
the waters. "This is Lucy."

Christy sat up, her lungs flaring as if a wave had
reached up high on the beach and washed over her.
She had figured that if she was lucky, her nieces would,
sometime, send her a text or an email. But she hadn't
expected a call. "Lucy! Hi!"

"Hi. Um—I guess I got your email?"

"Yes! Yes, I did send you an email." Grappling with
surprise, Christy searched for words. "Lucy—I'm so
glad you're calling. I was hoping we could talk."

"Sure. Um. We can talk." The older of Christy's two
nieces cleared her throat.

"I want to apologize, darling." The words tumbled out
of Christy's mouth.

"For what?" Now it was Lucy who sounded surprised.

"For...everything."

"Are you still there, Aunt Christy?"

"Yes, I am. I'm in the yard. Let me go into the house."
Christy rose from her towel. Luckily, she had already

thrown a white cotton dress over her swimsuit to prevent sunburn.

Beside her, Ethan rolled on his side on the picnic blanket and propped himself on an elbow. He took off his sunglasses, his eyes asking her if she wanted him to come. Christy shook her head; this conversation she had to have on her own. He nodded and smiled at her. Smiling back though her heart was pattering nervously in her chest, Christy walked up the new stone path to the cottage, brushing the sand off her.

"Are you still in San Francisco, Aunt Christy?"

Christy let herself into the cottage but left the door open. Inside, it was cool. The bright sunlight was tempered into a golden shimmer on the soft wood of the floors as she walked into the living room and sat on the soft new couch. "I moved just recently. Now I live in Mendocino Cove. It's a small seaside town a few hours up north, where the redwood forests grow."

"Really?" Lucy was much more audible now. "I think I've heard of Mendocino Cove. Isn't that where Ethan Conway lives?"

Christy drew in a deep breath. Did her nieces know that she and Abby had fallen out over Ethan? "He does. He and I...we met again. And, darling...he told me about your mom."

"Like what? What did he tell you?" Lucy's voice turned weary.

"He told me she struggled," Christy said gently. "All these years, I had no idea. I'm so terribly sorry I wasn't a better sister. And a better aunt."

"It's all right." Lucy hummed something else, but Christy didn't catch the words.

"It's not all right. I—"

"No. Aunt Christy, I'm serious. It's all right. Mom didn't want to stay in touch with anyone. It had nothing to do with kissing Ethan, if that's what you think." Lucy sighed.

"So you know about that?"

"Yeah. Mom liked to talk when she was...a bit of a mess." Lucy cleared her throat. "She was in and out of rehab, Aunt Christy. She didn't want you or her old friends to know. Lots of reasons, but I think she wanted someone to remember her the way she was before."

"Oh, sweetheart." It broke Christy's heart. "If Abby didn't want me, at least I should have been there for you."

"I mean, you were. It wasn't like we couldn't call you."

"Why didn't you?"

"I don't know. What could you have done? It's not like we were adrift, Aunt Christy. We always had Dad and his parents. He took us to England even before Mom..." She stopped talking abruptly.

Christy frowned. "Are you okay?"

"I just wanted to tell you that Dad passed away two weeks ago. I have to be honest; we didn't see it coming. He felt like he had a cold, and three months later... It was really fast." She swallowed tears, the sound audible across the many miles that separated them.

"I'm so sorry." Christy wanted to know what had happened, but it wasn't for her to pry. Besides, clearly,

Lucy was barely keeping it together. "Where are you now, sweetheart?"

"We're still in England, Maya and me. I don't know what we're going to do now. I feel sort of adrift." She cleared her throat a couple of times. "After you wrote, I told Maya I'd get in touch with you because you're the only family we have left. At least we should be on speaking terms."

Christy's thoughts were racing. "Listen, Lucy, I know I can't ask anything of you, but I'm wondering whether you and your sister would like to come visit? We're having beautiful weather here in Northern California; it's warm and sunny, and everything is in bloom. I just bought a cottage by the sea, and I have two guest rooms that are waiting for you two. Or, if you don't want to stay with me, I can get you rooms at the local hotel in town. It's a historic mansion that's very beautiful and..." She stopped herself, aware that she was rambling. "I'd just really like to see you two. I can't turn back time, but I want to make it up to you as best as I can."

"Are you serious?" Lucy didn't sound like she believed her aunt. "Do you mean it?"

"Yes! Yes, I'm very serious. I'd love to see you. I'd love to connect. I'd love to get to know my nieces."

"Um. Well...it sounds like a lovely place, and Ethan is forever telling us to come visit. But we hardly know each other. I'm not sure it's polite to invite ourselves into your home."

"It was me who invited you! Please come if you possibly can." Christy took a deep breath. "You are all I have for a family too."

"What if our visits overlap with any friends who might want to visit you?"

Christy felt a warm wave of hope rise inside her chest. "Don't worry about that, my dear. There is room for you in the cottage," she said. "And by the way, Ethan's house also has more spare bedrooms than he'll ever need."

"Oh, does he?"

There was enough interest in her niece's voice to make Christy bold. "Listen, I'll just send you airline tickets, shall I? You and your sister come if you want to, and if not, no worries. I haven't exactly been the aunt of the year. Of *any* year."

"You don't have to do that, Aunt Christy. Send tickets, I mean."

"I want to. Please? For all the...all the birthdays I missed." Christy's voice almost broke, thinking about all that she'd missed. "And the Christmases, and Easters.... it's little enough."

"Isn't it way too expensive?" The question came carefully, tentative, on tiptoes and eager not to offend.

Christy smiled. "No, it's not, Lucy. It would be my pleasure." She took a deep breath, hoping not to spook her niece by being too pushy. "What would be a good time for a visit? When can you come?"

"Um. I guess now? Maya was let go from her job for taking time off for Dad, and I'm not going to go to uni this semester. There's nowhere we have to be right now."

"Then come. I'll send you tickets, and you'll stay with me. We'll cook dinner together and have bonfires and walk on the beach... I have a little beach! The water is cold, but if you're brave, you can still swim."

"Really?" Lucy sounded a little more cheerful, a little more like she believed this was going to happen. "It sounds peaceful. But I didn't mean to fish for an invitation, Aunt Christy. I really just wanted to see how you are."

"I'd be much better if you'd come visit me." Christy smiled. Her poor nieces were obviously in need of Mendocino's healing powers. "Come visit and bring your sister. I'd love nothing more than to have you two visit."

"Well then...okay." Lucy chuckled softly. "It's funny. I don't even know what you look like now. Are you still working for that auction house?"

"I'm recently retired," Christy said. "I'm renovating my cottage, and I'm learning how to bake and take care of my garden. I have friends here in town, and, uh...I suppose I'm dating Ethan."

"Really?" For the first time, there was a smile in Lucy's voice. "So it all came full circle? A real second-chance romance?"

"You could call it that." Christy wanted to keep her niece on the phone forever, to ask all the questions she'd never asked.

"Good for you; Ethan's always been super nice. Listen, I hear the doorbell. I think it's Maya coming back from the market, and it's raining. Spring takes forever to come. I'd better go let her in."

"Tell her hi from me," Christy said. "And let me know how she feels about visiting. I'll look at flights and send you an email, okay?"

"Okay. Thanks, Aunt Christy. It was nice talking to you, and it'd be good to get out. I'll be in touch." Lucy ended the call.

Christy let her phone sink. The door to the garden opened and shut, and she heard Ethan walk through the house.

Dressed in jeans and a T-shirt but still barefoot and messy-haired from the beach, he leaned against the wall. "Who was that?" He frowned. "Is everything okay?"

Christy looked up. Her face felt flushed, and she pressed a hand to her warm cheek. "That was Lucy," she said softly. "Her dad passed away. The girls feel adrift, and I think..."

Ethan's frown disappeared, and he came over to her, sitting beside her on the couch. "What do you think, Christy?"

She looked at him. "I think they'll come visit. I invited Lucy, and she'll talk with Maya. I think..." She straightened her back as it sank in. "I really think they'll come!"

Something fluttered over Ethan's face; a shadow of the past, relief, a new hope. In a few strides, he closed the distance between them and pulled Christy into his arms, pressing his face in her hair. "I'm so glad," he murmured. "If you and the girls reconnect, I'll die a happy man."

Christy lightly slapped his back. "Don't talk about dying, Ethan. We have no time for that. We need to get the rooms upstairs ready for the girls."

"Girls." He smiled, cradling her face in his hands. "You realize they're grown women, don't you?"

Christy remembered them as young teens, with braids and braces. She'd not seen them since then. But now, she would. They would finally get to know each other, and she'd watch over them as best she could. "Well, then we have to get to work even more. I'm not going to put a grown woman in a guestroom without billowing curtains, vases full of flowers, or a good mattress on the bed." Christy kissed Ethan, and then she stood, plans tumbling through her head like unruly toddlers. "I'm going to go buy beds for all the guest rooms. Right now. And curtains. All upstairs windows need new curtains. And I need a lot more vases for flowers and...and all the things to make the girls feel comfortable and cared for."

Ethan laughed and stood as well. "Then I guess I'd better go get my truck and be your driver, my love. Lucky for you, it's part of my job to know all the good furniture stores. And while we're out and about, I'll take the opportunity to take you to a nice lunch." Smiling, he bent down and kissed her. "It's all coming together, isn't it?" he murmured, his lips brushing hers.

Christy smiled and kissed him back. "Yes," she said, joy and happiness and relief and love washing through her in a rising tide. "It all comes together now. I'm so glad."

Thank you so much for reading the Mendocino Cove Series! For a short bonus story, go to https://BookH ip.com/NGVXPMX and find out what happens next Lukas and Barbara. You can also return to beautiful Mendocino in the Mendocino Beach Series!

Mendocino Beach Series

Follow three friends into the captivating world of Mendocino Beach, where wonderful characters find support, romance, and second chances amidst the stunning coastal scenery. From heartwarming friendships to unexpected adventures, this feel-good sisterhood saga entertains and enchants until the very end!

BEACH COVE SERIES

★★★★★ *"What an awesome series! Captivated in the first sentence! Beautiful writing!"*

Maisie returns to charming Beach Cove and meets a heartwarming cast of old friends and new neighbors. The beaches are sandy and inviting, the sea is bluer than it should be, and the small town is brimming with big secrets. Together, Maisie and her sisters of the heart take turns helping each other through trials, mysteries, and matters of the heart. You can also get the free prequel to the series when you go to the link on Nellie's Facebook page!

BAY HARBOR BEACH SERIES

★★★★★ *"Wonderfully written story. Rumors abound in this tale of loves and secrets."*

Lose yourself in this riveting feel-good saga of old secrets and new beginnings. Best friends support each other through life's ups and downs and matters of the heart as they boil salt water taffy, browse quaint stores for swimsuits, and sample pies at the Beach Bistro!

ABOUT THE AUTHOR

Nellie Brooks writes feel-good friendship fiction for women. In her books you'll find flawed, likable characters who bake and adopt animals, gorgeous coastal settings that will make you study your tea leaves for the next vacation date, secrets that are best solved together, and happy endings until every estranged friend and distant sister is safe in the arms of her small town community.

Visit www.nelliebrooks.com to subscribe to her newsletter and hear about releases, promos, and writing news! You can also follow Nellie on Facebook and BookBub.

Made in United States
North Haven, CT
08 August 2024

55818119R00155